*For Jim and Barbara Hendry
of Golspie, Sutherland*

CRITICAL ACCLAIM FOR
M. C. BEATON'S HAMISH MACBETH
SERIES

Also by M. C. Beaton

DEATH OF A GOSSIP
DEATH OF A CAD
DEATH OF A PERFECT WIFE
DEATH OF AN OUTSIDER
DEATH OF A HUSSY
DEATH OF A PRANKSTER
DEATH OF A GLUTTON

and published by Bantam Books

DEATH OF
A SNOB

M.C. Beaton

BANTAM BOOKS
LONDON · NEW YORK · TORONTO · SYDNEY · AUCKLAND

DEATH OF A SNOB

A BANTAM BOOK : 0 553 40968 9

First publication in Great Britain

PRINTING HISTORY
Bantam edition published 1996

Set in 11pt Linotype Times by Kestrel Data, Exeter

Bantam Books are published by Transworld Publishers Ltd,
61–63 Uxbridge Road, Ealing, London W5 5SA,
in Australia by Transworld Publishers (Australia) Pty Ltd,
15–25 Helles Avenue, Moorebank, NSW 2170,
and in New Zealand by Transworld Publishers (NZ) Ltd,
3 William Pickering Drive, Albany, Auckland.

Reproduced, printed and bound in Great Britain by
Cox & Wyman Ltd, Reading, Berks.

CHAPTER ONE

Heap on more wood! – the wind is chill;
But let it whistle as it will;
We'll keep our Christmas merry still.
—SIR WALTER SCOTT

Police Constable Hamish Macbeth was a desperate man – ill, friendless, and, at the approach to Christmas, near to death.

Or so he told himself.

The start of the misery had been the beginning of a Scottish winter which seemed hell-bent on proving any scientist believing in the greenhouse effect a fool. Like many others in the village of Lochdubh on the west coast of Sutherland, Hamish had contracted a severe cold with all its attendant miseries of boiling head, running nose, aching joints, and monumental self-pity. Although he had not phoned anyone to tell of his misery, nevertheless, like all people in the grip of self-pity, he expected his friends to have telepathic powers.

The only bright spark in all the gloom was that he was going home for Christmas. His parents had moved to a croft house and land near Rogart. He would soon be there, with his mother to fuss over him.

He was hunched up in his bed. He was hungry and thirsty but could not be bothered getting up to get himself anything. His dog Towser, a yellowish mongrel, lay stretched out at the end of his bed, snoring happily and apparently as indifferent as the rest of Lochdubh to the long lank bundle of misery that was PC Macbeth.

The wind of Sutherland, always savage, had taken on a new dark intensity and boomed down the sea loch outside, bearing long snaking writhing arms of fine snow, tearing at the fabric of the house, yelling and shouting in triumph.

And then suddenly, the phone in the police-station office began to ring, sharp and insistent. He hoped no-one had committed a crime. He felt too ill to cope, but if he did not attend to the matter himself, Sergeant MacGregor would have to travel all the way from Cnothan, and the peeved sergeant would then set about making trouble for him at police headquarters in Strathbane. He shoved his feet into a battered pair of carpet slippers and, snivelling dismally, he went through to the cold office and picked up the phone.

'Hamish,' came his mother's voice, 'I've got bad news.'

His heart gave a lurch. 'Are you all right?' he asked. 'Nothing up with Faither?'

'No, no, son. It's about Christmas.'

'What about Christmas?' Hamish had a bleak

feeling that whatever his mother had to tell him about Christmas was not going to cheer him one bit.

'Well, Aunt Hannah's coming all the way from America. Sprung it on us at the last minute.'

Hamish gripped the phone and stifled a sneeze. Aunt Hannah was a fat, loud-mouthed harridan who loathed Hamish. But she had been generous to the not-too-comfortably-off Macbeths with presents of money and gifts for Hamish's little brothers and sisters. Never anything for Hamish. She loathed him and never tired of saying so.

His mother's voice grew plaintive, 'So you see, son, after all Hannah's done for us and her coming all this way to see us . . .'

There was another long silence.

At last Hamish said bleakly, 'You don't want me to come.' It was not a question.

'I knew you'd understand,' pleaded his mother. 'I mean, it's only this one Christmas. You could come at the New Year when she's gone.'

'Aye, all right,' muttered Hamish.

'I mean,' coaxed Mrs Macbeth, 'you've got lots o' friends in Lochdubh. Your voice sounds funny.'

'I haff got the influenza,' said Hamish, his Highland accent growing more sibilant, a sure sign he was upset.

'Och,' said Mrs Macbeth with all the heartlessness of a busy mother with a large family, 'you always did think you were dying when you got a wee bit o' a cold. Take some aspirin and go to bed.'

Another silence. 'Wass there anything else?'

Hamish finally asked in accents as chilly as the police office.

'No, no, that was all. Sorry, son, but you know how Hannah is. Ever since you put that mouse down her back when you were eight, she's never been fond o' you. The new house is just fine. Rare and warm. The fires draw just grand.'

'When's Aunt Hannah arriving?' asked Hamish.

'On the twentieth.'

'Provided I am still alive,' said Hamish stiffly, 'I'll run over with your presents before then.'

'Aye, that'll be great. See you then.'

Hamish shuffled back miserably to bed. No-one wanted him. He was alone in the world. He was dying and nobody cared.

There came a sharp rap at the back door. He sneezed dismally and stayed where he was. Towser stirred lazily and slowly wagged his tail. The rapping came louder now, more peremptory.

Hamish's conscience gave him a nudge. He was Lochdubh's only policeman, the weather was savage, and someone out there might be in trouble. He groaned as he got up again, slung an old woollen dressing-gown about his shoulders, and made his way to the kitchen door.

He opened it and Priscilla Halburton-Smythe was borne in on a gust of wind and snow.

'Oh, it's yerself, Priscilla,' said Hamish.

Priscilla, once the love of his life, until Hamish had grown heartily sick of the weight of the torch he was carrying for her, slammed the door on the storm and looked at Hamish.

'I know crime's thin on the ground here at the best of times,' she said briskly, 'but it's two in the afternoon and you've obviously just got out of bed.'

'I am a sick man,' said Hamish furiously, 'but a fat lot you care. You never even thought to phone.'

'How on earth was I supposed to know you were sick?' asked Priscilla. She looked slowly around the kitchen, at the cold stove, at the dirty pots and dishes piled up in the sink. 'This place is enough to make anyone ill. For heaven's sake, get back to bed and leave me to clear up this mess.'

'Couldn't you chust make us a cup of tea and come and sit by the bed and talk to me?' moaned Hamish.

'Nonsense. You'll feel miles better when this place is spick and span.' Priscilla radiated nervous energy. She had grown thin and spare and her hair was scraped up in an untidy knot on the top of her head. Hamish thought that since her family home, Tommel Castle, had been turned into an hotel, she had not once relaxed. Although her father, Colonel Halburton-Smythe, owned the hotel, all the work fell on Priscilla. As there was excellent fishing and shooting, it was busy even in winter. It was Priscilla who saw to everything, from ordering the food and drink to soothing down the guests offended by her father's blunt manner. In an amazingly short time, she had made a success of the business, but she had lost her cool good looks and graceful movements; perpetually worried, perpetually strung up, now brittle to snapping point.

Hamish crept back to bed. 'What a pigsty!' exclaimed Priscilla, following him in. 'Have you fed Towser?'

'Just some o' the hard food. He doesnae like it owermuch.'

'He never did like it. He likes people food. You know that, Hamish. Come, Towser.'

Towser slid off the bed and crept servilely after her.

Hamish lay listening to the sound of Priscilla scrubbing floors and cleaning out cupboards and washing dishes. He felt she ought to be at his bedside, stroking his brow, instead of going on like some sort of health visitor.

Two hours later, she crashed into the bedroom, carrying a bucket and mop and dusters. She raked out the fire, which was choked with cold ashes, piled it up with paper and wood, and set a cheerful blaze crackling. 'I've run you a hot bath,' she said over her shoulder. 'Go and take it while I change your bed.'

'I think I'm too ill to take a bath.'

'Take it,' she ordered, 'and stop being so disgustingly sorry for yourself.'

'Haff I complained?' Hamish gave her thin back a wounded look.

'You are exuding such self-pity, it's creeping like smoke through the whole place. *Go on!*'

Injured, Hamish stalked off to the bathroom. With quick nervous movements, Priscilla stripped the sheets off the bed and replaced them with clean ones. She dusted and vacuumed the room and then made up a flask of tea and put it, along with a cup, at Hamish's bedside.

Hamish emerged from his bath to find Priscilla waiting to settle him in bed. She neatly arranged the blankets over him and then tucked them in all round him, so firmly he felt he was in a strait-jacket.

'There's tea in that flask,' said Priscilla, 'and a casserole on the stove for your dinner. Towser's been fed.'

Hamish wriggled his toes and eased the tight blankets a bit. The fire was roaring up the chimney and the room looked clean and comfortable and there was a delicious smell coming from the kitchen. He began to feel better.

'I'd better be off,' sighed Priscilla. 'I didn't mean to be here so long.'

'Thank you,' said Hamish awkwardly, and then blurted out before he could stop himself, 'My, lassie, but you're awf'y thin.'

Priscilla sat down on the end of the bed. 'I know,' she said. 'And to think that before Daddy started the hotel, I was considering going on a diet.'

'If he looks after the money this time instead of handing it over to some con man,' – Priscilla winced, said con man having been one of her boy-friends – 'he should be able to take down that hotel sign soon and return to being a private landowner.'

'He enjoys it all,' said Priscilla sadly. 'He's having the time of his life.'

'Yes, I have seen him.' Hamish looked at her sympathetically. 'You run yourself ragged with all

13

the management and bookings and complaints while he puts on a black tie in the evening and lords it over the guests. Then he has a few and forgets they're paying guests and is nasty to them, and you have to soothe them down.'

'I'll manage.'

'You don't need to,' said Hamish. 'Things are going just fine. Why, he could hire an experienced hotel manager and give you a break.'

'But no-one else could handle the guests the way I can,' protested Priscilla.

'Once the colonel was paying someone to run things, he might mind his tongue. It's because you're his daughter and a woman that he treats you like a skivvy.'

'It's not as bad as that.' Priscilla rose to go.

'Well, it was nice of you to come and look after me.'

Priscilla turned pink. 'I didn't know you were ill, Hamish. There's another reason.'

'Oh, aye? I should hae known,' he said huffily. 'Out with it.'

'There's this friend of mine staying at the hotel. She's leaving at the end of the week. She's got a bit of a problem and doesn't want to go to the police direct, if you know what I mean. She just wants some advice. Could you see her? I'd rather she told you about it.'

'Oh, all right. Bring her down tomorrow. What's her name?'

'Jane. Jane Wetherby.'

* * *

14

The next day, the snow stopped and a mild gale blew in from the Atlantic, turning the snow to slush. For a brief few hours, a watery sunlight shone on the choppy waters of the loch before night fell, as it does in the far north of Scotland in winter, at two in the afternoon.

Hamish was feeling considerably better. He received a phone call from headquarters at Strathbane reminding him that he was expected to stop motorists at random and breathalyse them as part of a campaign to stop drunk driving over Christmas. Hamish, who knew every drunk in the village and solved the problem by taking their car keys away, had no intention of wasting time breathalysing the rest of the population.

He ate lunch, fed his hens, gave his sheep their winter feed, and then climbed back into bed with a book. He had completely forgotten about Priscilla's friend. Lulled by a glass of toddy, his eyes were beginning to close when he heard a car driving up.

Then he remembered about Jane Wetherby. It was too late to get dressed. He rose and tied his dressing-gown about him and made for the kitchen door, exuding a strong smell of whisky and wintergreen.

'Be back for Jane later,' called Priscilla. 'I'll leave you to it.'

Hamish ushered Jane into the kitchen and then looked at her in startled amazement as she removed her coat and threw it on a kitchen chair. She was a tall woman wearing a brief divided skirt in shocking-pink wool, and her long, long legs ended in high-heeled sandals with thin patent-leather straps. Her thin white blouse plunged at the front to a deep V. Hamish cast a wild look through the kitchen window as if to reassure himself that the weather had not turned tropical, and then took in the rest of her. She had cloudy dark hair and very large grey-green eyes, a straight thin nose, and a long thin upper lip over a small pouting lower lip.

'Well, well,' said Jane in a sort of breathy voice, 'so you're the village constable. Why aren't you in uniform?'

'Because,' retorted Hamish sharply, 'I am very sick. Did Priscilla no' tell you?'

She shook her head. 'Come ben, then,' said Hamish sulkily. Here he was, at death's door, and Priscilla had not even bothered to tell her friend he was sick. He began to feel shaky and ill again. Priscilla had left the living-room fire set with paper and logs. He struck a match and lit it.

Jane sank down into an armchair and crossed her long legs.

'The trouble,' she said, suddenly leaning forward so that her blouse plunged alarmingly low at the front, 'is that you are not going the right way about curing your cold. It is the common cold, isn't it?'

Hamish, now in the armchair opposite, took out a handkerchief and blew his nose miserably by way of reply.

'It is all in your mind,' said Jane. 'The weather has been very cold and so you began to feel

16

you might get one and your mind conveyed that message to the rest of your body and so you got one. Put your index fingers on either side of your head, just at the temples, and repeat after me, concentrating all the while, "I have not got a cold. I am fit and well."'

'Havers,' said Hamish crossly.

'There you have it,' said Jane triumphantly. 'You have just told me what I had already guessed.'

'That you were havering?' commented Hamish rudely.

'No, no. That you *want* to have a cold and make everyone feel sorry for you.' She leaned back and uncrossed and crossed her legs. Embarrassed, Hamish looked at the ceiling.

'What is the difficulty you're in?' Hamish asked the lampshade. He found those flashing legs and thighs unnerving.

'I think someone might be trying to kill me.'

Hamish's hazel eyes focused on her. 'Did you tell someone else how to get rid of their cold?'

'Do be serious. Oh, perhaps I am imagining it, but a rock did hurtle down last week close to my head, and then there was the bathroom heater. I had run my bath and was just about to step into it when the wall heater came tumbling down, right into the bath. I called in a local builder, but he said the heater had probably just come loose as the plaster was damp.'

'Did you think of telling the local policeman?'

'The local policeman is Sandy Ferguson. Have you heard of him?'

'Yes,' said Hamish, remembering the famous day in Strathbane when Sandy Ferguson, drunk as usual, had told Detective Chief Inspector Blair exactly what he thought of him and had been subsequently banished to the Hebrides. 'Never say you're living on Eileencraig!'

Jane nodded.

'You'd better begin at the beginning,' said Hamish.

Jane looked doubtfully at the thin, red-haired constable in the old dressing-gown and then made up her mind.

'I run a health farm called The Happy Wanderer . . .'

'Oh, my.' Hamish winced.

'Called The Happy Wanderer,' went on Jane firmly, 'on the island of Eileencraig. Part of the healthy regime is brisk walking. I decided to go into business for myself after my divorce two years ago. It had been pretty successful. Health farms are the coming thing. I not only teach people how to have a healthy body but how to get in touch with their innermost feelings. Do you read me?'

'Sort of.'

'Well, the islanders are a clannish lot and don't like incomers, so I thought perhaps the rock thingie and the heater thingie were, well, *pranks* to scare me away. That was until I spoke to Mrs Bannerman at Skulag, the main village, and she read my tea-leaves and she saw death in them. Someone from far away was trying to kill me, she said. That's when I began to worry about my guests.'

'Paying guests?'

'No, the health farm is closed for the winter. Friends.'

'Who are these friends?'

'People I invited to spend Christmas with me. There's a Mr and Mrs Todd from Glasgow, he's in real estate; then there's Harriet Shaw, the writer.'

'Haven't heard of her,' commented Hamish.

'*You* wouldn't. She writes cookery books. There's Sheila and Ian Carpenter from Yorkshire – dear, dear people, he's a farmer.' Jane threw back her head and gave a merry laugh. She's practised that laugh in front of the mirror, thought Hamish suddenly. 'And,' said Jane, suddenly looking solemn, 'there's my ex.'

'Your ex-husband?'

'Yes, John. He's been working so hard. He does need a holiday.'

'Who divorced whom?'

The large eyes opposite shifted away from him slightly. 'Oh, we were very civilized about it. A mutual agreement. Well, there you are. What do you think?'

'Are they still there?'

'Oh, yes. After what Mrs Bannerman saw in the tea-leaves, I felt I had to get away to meditate and heard Priscilla had fallen on hard times and so I thought I would hop over for a couple of nights just to *think*. What do *you* think?'

'First of all,' said Hamish, 'I believe Eileencraig is a weird enough place to give anyone the jitters. You're right. They hate incomers. I think the heater and the rock were plain and simple accidents. But when the villagers heard you were going to visit Mrs Bannerman to get your fortune told, they must have put her up to giving you a fright. That, in my opinion, is all there is to it.'

She leaned forward and the blouse plunged alarmingly again. 'Do you know,' said Jane in that breathy, sexy voice of hers, 'you are a *most* intelligent man.' She threw back her head and gave that practised merry laugh of hers again. 'I was so edgy that when Priscilla told me about you, I was going to invite you to come back with me for Christmas and bribe you with the promise of an old-fashioned dinner of turkey and mince pies.'

Hamish sat stricken. Then he said carefully, 'On the other hand, I cannot help thinking about my Aunt Hannah, her that lives in San Francisco.'

'Yes?'

'She always swore she would neffer set foot in Scotland again, but a wee woman in the Chinese quarter told her fortune and said she would soon be going on a long journey to her native land. She forgot all about it, until one day she found she had booked a plane flight home to Scotland. Then there wass ma cousin Jamie . . .'

Jane's mouth fell a little open as she gazed at him.

'Yes, Jamie,' said Hamish in a crooning voice. 'He was at this game fair and a gypsy woman had a caravan there. Jamie and his friends had a wee bit too much to drink and they urged Jamie to have his tea-leaves read. Into that black caravan he went,

20

laughing something awful and telling that gypsy woman it was all a load of rubbish. But she read the leaves.'

'And?' urged Jane, who was goggling at him.

'And the gypsy woman said, "Laugh ye may, but look out for your life. Next week, someone is going to try to kill you." Well, Jamie, he thought she was trying to get revenge because he had laughed at her, but the very next week' – Hamish lowered his voice to a whisper – 'he wass in Aberdeen, looking for work on the rigs and someone mugged him.'

'No!'

'Oh, yes, and stuck a knife in his side. He's lucky to be alive.'

'I have never jeered at the paranormal,' said Jane. 'You may think me foolish, Hamish, but I am begging you now to come with me. Can you get any leave?'

'I happen to be on leave as from tomorrow,' said Hamish, 'but with this cold . . .'

'I have very good central heating,' said Jane, 'and you will be looked after like a king.'

'Seeing as how you are a friend of Priscilla's, I'll force myself to go,' said Hamish.

When Priscilla arrived to pick Jane up, she looked amazed to hear that Hamish intended to travel to Eileencraig with Jane and stay there for Christmas. 'I'll talk to you later,' said Priscilla.

Jane's eyes fell on Towser. 'No dogs,' she said.

'Perhaps I can take Towser.' Priscilla looked doubtful. 'But I'll talk to you later, Hamish.'

After they had gone, Hamish poured himself a celebratory whisky. He had nearly blown it. If he had not invented those tales about his relatives and the tea-leaves, he might not have had a comfortable Christmas to look forward to.

Priscilla arrived that evening, looking cross. 'What on earth are you up to, Hamish Macbeth? Jane told me some rubbish about tea-leaves and I was leaving it to you to talk her out of it. Besides, what will your family think?'

'They don't want me,' said Hamish. 'Aunt Hannah's coming over from the States and that means I have to stay away. She cannae stand me. Och, I forgot the presents for the family. I was supposed to take them over at the end of the week.'

He looked at Priscilla pleadingly.

'All right! All right!' she said impatiently. 'I'll take Towser *and* the presents over to Rogart. In fact, I'll do it tomorrow and get it over with. There's bad weather forecast. The wind's turned to the east and all that slush is beginning to freeze like mad. I can't help feeling guilty about letting you trick Jane into that invitation, but seeing as how you've got a holiday and nowhere else to go, and seeing as how Jane is simply loaded, I suppose it should be all right.'

'You're always rushing.' Hamish tried to take her coat. 'Sit down for a bit.'

'No, no, I daren't. We've got a party of Spanish aristocrats. They speak perfect English, which is something Daddy refuses to understand, so he shouts at them and thinks if he puts *h* in front of everything, he's speaking Spanish. You should hear him roaring, 'H'everything h'OK?'

She threw her arms about him and gave him an impulsive hug. 'Be good, Hamish. Have a merry Christmas.'

'Merry Christmas,' echoed Hamish as she hurtled out of the door and banged it behind her. He could still feel the warmth of her thin body for a few moments after she had gone, and into his mind came slight, sad, bitter-sweet memories of the days when he had loved her so much.

The sun came up at ten in the morning to shine over a glittering icy landscape, a glaring yellow sun which forecast high gales to come. True to her promise, Priscilla collected Towser and the presents and set out on the long road to Rogart while Hamish climbed into Jane's Range Rover and headed down the coast. Jane said that a fishing boat would take them out to the island, as no passenger ferry was due there for another week. She was wearing a short leather jerkin over another short skirt and a pair of black leather thigh-boots. She discoursed at length on her innermost feelings as she drove competently down the winding twisty roads beside the glittering sea. If anyone ever issued a press handout about innermost feelings, it would read rather like Jane's conversation, reflected Hamish. She suffered, she said, from low self-esteem and a perpetual feeling of insecurity, and Hamish wondered if she really felt anything much at all. She seemed to be reciting something she had read about someone else rather than talking about herself. He wished suddenly he had not taken her up on her invitation. It would have been fun if he could have gone to his parents' instead with Priscilla. He had not seen much of Priscilla of late. She was always busy, always rushing.

Priscilla drove under the shadow of the towering Sutherland mountains. Great gusts of wind tore at the car and then the snow began to fall. She switched on her headlights and leaned forward, peering through the driving snow, watching the road in front uneasily as it became whiter and whiter. She heaved a sigh of relief when at last she saw the orange street lights of Lairg ahead. Not far to go.

The road from Lairg to Rogart is quite a good one, although it seemed, that afternoon, to be disappearing rapidly under the snow. Priscilla stopped outside Rogart and studied a map Hamish had drawn for her. The Macbeths' house was above the village, up on the hills.

She was feeling tired with the strain of driving so long in the howling blizzard. She crawled up the hill road at the back of Rogart, peering anxiously in front of her. And then, with great relief, she saw the telephone-box that Hamish had drawn at a crossroads on his map. The entrance to the croft was a few yards up on the left. The car groaned and chugged its way along. She had almost decided she would need to stop and get out and walk when she dimly saw the low shape of a white croft house. Hoping she was not driving across the front garden, she drew up outside the door and sat for a moment, rubbing her tired eyes.

The kitchen door opened and the small round figure of Hamish's mother appeared. 'It's yourself, Priscilla,' she cried in amazement. 'And the dog! Where's Hamish?'

'It's a long story,' said Priscilla, climbing out of the car and walking with Towser into the welcoming warmth of the house. There seemed to be Macbeths everywhere, both large and small, and all with Hamish's flaming-red hair.

'I'll just leave Towser and the presents from Hamish, and then I'd better get back,' said Priscilla, after explaining where Hamish was.

'Nonsense,' said Mrs Macbeth. 'Sit yourself down, lassie. You're no' going anywhere tonight.'

She was hustled into the living-room and pressed down into a battered armchair by the fire. A glass of whisky was put into her hand. Priscilla realized for the first time in months that she was tired, bone-tired. Her eyes began to droop and the empty glass was gently removed from her hand. Soon she was fast asleep.

'Did ye ever see such a mess o' skin and bone?' said Mrs Macbeth, looking down at Priscilla. 'It's fattening up that lassie needs. She cannae go anywhere until the roads are clear. And it's just as well. Hamish said that faither o' hers was a slave-driver, horrible wee man that he is. I think we'll keep her here for a bit until she gets some rest.'

Mr Macbeth smiled at her vaguely and retreated behind his newspaper. He had given up arguing with his wife exactly two weeks after they were married.

'I do rely on Priscilla for advice,' Jane was saying as she drove competently along a stone jetty. 'We'll just wait in the car until we see the boat coming, Hamish, and then I'll garage it in that lock-up over there. Yes, Priscilla. So cool. Such a relaxing girl. Oh, there's the boat.'

Hamish climbed out of the warmth of the Range Rover and shivered on the jetty. Small pellets of snow were beginning to blow through the rising wind. He looked over the sea and experienced a slight feeling of uneasiness, almost dread, and wished he had not come.

CHAPTER TWO

From the lone shieling of the misty island
Mountains divide us and the waste of seas –
Yet still the blood is strong, the heart is Highland,
And we in dreams behold the Hebrides!
—Sir Walter Scott

The lights of the fishing boat which was to carry them to Eileencraig bobbed closer across the water. Hamish, out of uniform, pulled his tweed-coat collar up against the biting wind. Jane, he noticed, was wearing her jacket open. There might be something to this health-farm business after all, he thought.

The fisherman was a gnarled little man with a sour expression. Jane hailed him gaily, but he jumped nimbly on to the jetty and began to tie the rope around a bollard, ignoring her completely, as did his second in command, a pimply-faced boy with pale eyes, a wet mouth, and an incipient beard.

'Angus is quite a character,' said Jane, meaning the fisherman and giving that merry laugh of hers again. She and Hamish went on board, Hamish carrying her heavy suitcase and his own travelbag. The two-man crew cast off and the boat bucketed out over the rough sea. Hamish went down below to an oily, stinking little engine room furnished with two smelly berths and a dirty table. He sat on one of the berths. The youth scrambled down and went into the galley and put a kettle on the stove, which was lurching about on its gimbals.

'What's your name?' asked Hamish.

'Joseph Macleod,' said the boy. He began to whistle through his teeth.

'Is Mrs Wetherby in the wheel-house?' asked Hamish.

'Naw, herself is oot on the deck.'

'In this weather?'

'Aye, her's daft. There's worse coming.' The boat lurched and bucketed but the boy kept his balance, swaying easily with the erratic motion. 'Right bad storm inland. Heard it on the radio.'

Hamish thought uneasily of Priscilla. They were on the west coast. The storm had been driven in from the east. He hoped she was safe.

Jane clattered down to join Hamish, her face shining with good health. 'Marvellous sea,' she said. 'Waves like mountains.'

'I can feel them, and that's enough,' Hamish, still seated on one of the berths with the raised edge of it digging into his thighs, looked queasily at Jane. 'It's a wonder you got them to bring the boat out in this weather.'

'I pay well.' Jane lay down on the other berth and raised one booted leg in the air to admire it.

Hamish had to hand it to Jane. It was a dreadful crossing and yet she prattled on as if lying on a sofa in her own living-room. The little fishing boat crawled up one wave and plunged down the next and then wallowed about in the choppy trough at the bottom before scaling another watery mountain. The boy left the kettle and started to work the pumps, for sea water was crashing down the companion-way. The air was horrid with the sound of wind and waves and the groanings of the boat as it fought its way to Eileencraig.

Hamish's cold felt worse. His forehead was hot and there was a ringing in his ears. Jane's presence was claustrophobic. There was too much of everything about her, thought Hamish dizzily. Too much length of black-booted leg, too much cleavage, and too much of that breathy, sexy voice that rose remorselessly above the storm.

'The reason for the divorce,' Jane was saying, 'was that we both needed space. It's very important to have space in a marriage, don't you think?'

'I wouldn't know,' replied Hamish, 'not being married myself.'

Jane's large eyes swivelled round like headlamps turning a corner to focus on him. 'Everyone to their own bag,' she said cheerfully. 'Have you a lover?'

'I am not a homosexual.'

'Then why aren't you married? I mean, you're over thirty, aren't you? And anyone over thirty who is not married is either a homosexual or emotionally immature.'

'It could be argued that divorce is a sign of

29

emotional immaturity,' said Hamish. 'Inability to make a go of things once the first fine careless rapture has died down.'

'Why, Hamish Macbeth, you are straight out of the Dark Ages!'

Hamish got up and clutched at a shelf for support. 'Going to get a breath of air,' he said, and scurried up the iron stairs before Jane could volunteer to accompany him.

It was still wild, but the great seas were dying. He went into the wheel-house. 'Nearly there,' grunted the fisherman.

Hamish peered through the spray-blotched window. 'Can't see anything but darkness and water.'

'Ower there.' The fisherman pointed to the middle west. Hamish strained his eyes. He had never been to Eileencraig. Then, all at once, he saw lights in the blackness, lights so low that he seemed to be looking down on them. He was to find out later that a large part of the centre of the very flat island was below sea-level. The sea was calming. Somewhere far overhead, the wind was tearing and shrieking, but down below, all was suddenly still, an eerie effect, as if Eileencraig, like a sort of aquatic Brigadoon, had risen from the sea.

Jane appeared on deck, obviously looking for him. He went out to join her. The boat cruised into a wooden jetty. There were little knots of people standing on the jetty.

As they disembarked, Hamish carrying the luggage, he gave them a cheery salute of 'Afternoon,' but they all stared back at Hamish and Jane without moving, like sullen villagers in some long-forgotten war watching the arrival of their conquerors. There was something uncanny about their stillness, their watching. Their very clothes seemed to belong to an older age: the women in black shawls, the men in shiny tight suits. They stood immobile, watching, ever watching, not moving an inch, so that Hamish and Jane had to walk around the little groups to get off the jetty.

Hamish had once had a murder case in a Sutherland village called Cnothan. There, the inhabitants were anything but friendly but would have looked like a welcoming committee compared to these islanders.

Jane strode to where an ex-army jeep was parked and swung her long legs into it, and Hamish climbed in beside her after slinging the luggage into the back. 'Horrible old thing,' commented Jane, 'but sheer extravagance to leave anything more expensive lying around. They'd just take it to pieces.'

'Out of spite?' Hamish looked back at the islanders on the jetty, who had all turned around and were now staring at the jeep, their black silhouettes against the jetty lights, like cardboard cut-outs.

Jane drove off. 'Oh, no,' she shouted above the noise of the engine. 'They're rather sweet really. Just like naughty children.'

'Why on earth do you stay in such a place?'

'It is part of the health routine to have walks and exercise in such a remote, unspoiled part. My guests love it.'

They probably would, thought Hamish, cushioned as they were from the stark realities of remote island life.

'And just smell that air!'

As the jeep was an open one, there was little else Hamish could do but smell the air. The road wound through the darkness, the headlights picking out acres of bleak bog at every turn.

Jane swerved off the road and drove over a heathery track and then along the hard white sand of a curve of beach. 'There it is,' she called. 'At the end.'

Floodlit, The Happy Wanderer stood in all its glory, cocking a snoot at the simple grandeur of beach and moorland. It had been built like one of those pseudo-Spanish villas in California with arches and curved wrought-iron balconies, the whole having been painted white. A pink curly sign, 'The Happy Wanderer,' shone out into the blackness.

It fronted right on the beach. Jane pulled up at the entrance.

'Home at last,' she said. 'Come in, Hamish, and I'll show you to your room.'

The front door led straight into the main lounge. There was a huge fireplace filled with blazing logs; in front of it stood several chintz-covered sofas and armchairs. The room had a high arched wooden ceiling and fake skin rugs on the floor; a fake leopardskin lay in front of the fire, and nylon sheepskins dotted, like islands, the haircord carpet. Several modern paintings in acid colours swore from the walls. There was no reception desk, no receptionist, no pigeon-holes for keys and letters.

Jane conducted him down a corridor that led off the far end of the lounge and threw open a door with the legend 'Rob Roy' on it. The room was large, designed in a sort of 1970s interior decorator's shades of brown and cream, with a large vase of brown-and-cream dried flowers on a low glass table. There was a double bed and a desk and several chairs and a private bathroom. A bad painting of Rob Roy waving a broadsword and standing on his native heath looked down from over a strictly ornamental fireplace, and a book-shelf full of women's magazines was beside the bed. There was, however, no television; nor a phone.

'Where is everyone?' asked Hamish.

'I suppose they're in the television room as usual. Odd, isn't it? I mean the way people can't live without television.'

'Can I have my key?' asked Hamish.

Again that merry laugh, which was beginning to grate on Hamish's nerves. 'We don't have keys here, copper. No need for them. We're all one big happy family. I try to make it as much like a private house as possible.'

'Yes, and I suppose if anyone does pinch anything, they wouldn't get very far,' commented Hamish cynically. 'There's no phone, so I suppose there's no room service. Any chance o' a cup of tea?'

Jane looked at him seriously. 'Do you know that tea contains just as much caffeine as coffee?'

33

'Coffee would do just fine.'

'You don't understand. *Both* are bad for you. But come and meet the others when you're ready.'

Hamish sighed and sat down after she had left. He wondered whether he was supposed to change into black tie for dinner and then decided that the rugged people who came to remote, wind-swept health farms probably sat down in shorts and T-shirts.

He had a hot bath, changed into a clean shirt, sports jacket and flannels, swallowed two aspirin, and went in search of the others.

By following the sound of the six-o'clock news, he located the television room. Only one person looked up when he entered, a woman who had been reading a book. The rest were staring at the box. Jane then burst into the room. She had changed into a sort of white leather jump suit, the gold zip pulled down to reveal that cleavage. 'Drinks in the lounge,' she called.

A tetchy-looking man who held a remote control switched off the television. The small party rose stiffly to their feet. Hamish thought that they all, with the exception of the book-reading woman, looked as if they had been gazing at the television set since Jane had left on her visit to Priscilla.

A drinks trolley was pulled up near the fire. 'I'll introduce our newcomer,' said Jane. 'This is Hamish Macbeth, a friend of Priscilla's – you know Priscilla, the one I went to see. Hamish, first names will do. Heather and Diarmuid, Sheila and Ian, Harriet and John.'

Hamish's eyes roved over the group. Which was Jane's ex? He found the woman who had been reading had joined him. She had been introduced as Harriet. This then was Harriet Shaw, the cookery-book writer. She was a stylish-looking woman in her forties with a sallow, clever face made almost attractive by a pair of large humorous grey eyes.

'Jane told me you write books,' said Hamish.

'Yes,' said Harriet. 'I came up here in the hope of getting some old Scottish recipes from the islanders.'

Hamish looked rueful. 'I wouldn't bank on it. You'll find they dine on things like fish fingers and iced cakes made in Glasgow. Help me out. Who are the others? First names are not a help.'

'Have a drink first,' said Harriet.

'In a moment. I would really prefer a cup of tea. Jane seems down on caffeine, though. I thought she would have frowned on alcohol.'

'She seems to think it all right in moderation. Well, the couple drinking gin and tonics are Heather and Diarmuid Todd. He's in real estate. She's a self-appointed culture vulture.'

Diarmuid Todd was an attractive-looking man; that is, to anyone who liked the looks shown in tobacco advertisements. He had thick brown wavy hair and a pipe clenched between his teeth. He was smiling enigmatically and staring off into the middle distance. Despite the heat of the lounge, he was wearing a chunky Aran sweater with blue cords and boat shoes without socks.

His wife, Heather, looked older. She had blackish-brown hair and was wearing a pink jump suit with high heels. But her figure was lumpy and she looked like a parody of Jane, whom she obviously admired immensely. She had a doughy face set in lines of discontent.

'And Tweedledum and Tweedledee, that's Ian and Sheila Carpenter.'

Ian and Sheila Carpenter were both roly-poly people with fat jolly faces and fat jolly smiles. They were flirting with each other in a kittenish, affectionate way.

'The small, bad-tempered man is Jane's ex, John Wetherby.'

John was well-groomed, slightly plump, looking as if he had been reluctantly dragged from his office. He was wearing an immaculately tailored pin-striped suit, a shirt with a white separate collar and striped front, and an old school tie.

'He's a barrister,' said Harriet. 'So what do *you* do?'

Hamish hesitated. It was obvious that Jane did not want anyone to know he was a policeman. 'I work for the forestry,' he said.

Heather Todd, who had come up to them, caught Hamish's last remark. Her eyes bored insolently into his. 'Good heavens,' she said, 'where did Jane pick *you* up?'

'In Lochdubh, on the mainland,' said Hamish amiably.

Heather's voice was Glaswegian, although it would take a practised ear to register the fact.

Among the middle classes of Glasgow it had become unfashionable to try to affect an English accent, the painful result of that effort usually coming out as what was damned not so long ago as Kelvinside, the name of one of the posher areas, where glass came out as 'gless' and path as 'peth.' The new generation of middle-aged, middle-class snobs affected a transatlantic drawl ('I godda go') but occasionally throwing in a few chosen words of Scottish dialect to show they were of the people, there being nothing more snobbish than a left-wing Glaswegian who longed for the days when that city was a dump of slums and despair instead of having its present successful image. These same snobs talked about 'the workers' and their rights frequently, but made sure they never knew one, short of indulgently telling some barman when they were slumming to 'buy that wee fellow in the cap a drink.'

'Do you realize what you and your like are doing?' demanded Heather.

'No, tell me.' Hamish looked around, wondering whether he could ask Jane to relent and fetch him a cup of tea. There did not seem to be any staff.

'Covering the Highlands with those ghastly conifers, and all so that rich yuppies in England can get a tax shelter.'

'Forestry is no longer a tax shelter,' pointed out Hamish. 'There arnae that many jobs in the Highlands, and forestry's a blessing.'

'Well, that's not the way *I* see it,' said Heather, casting her eyes about her to draw an audience from the rest. 'The massacre of the flow country in Sutherland, the damage to the environment . . .' Her hectoring voice went on and on. Hamish did not like the dreary new pine forests that covered the north of Scotland, but someone like Heather always made him feel like defending them.

'I'll find you a cup of tea,' said Harriet's voice at his ear, and she tugged at his sleeve. They slipped quietly away while Heather continued her lecture, her eyes half-closed so that she could better enjoy the sound of her own voice, which went on and on.

Harriet led him into a sterile-looking kitchen where everything gleamed white under strips of fluorescent light.

'I bet it's herb tea,' said Hamish, looking gloomily about.

'No, real tea. I've been in charge of the kitchen while Jane's been away.' Harriet opened a cupboard and took down a canister of tea and then plugged in an eletric kettle.

'Never tell me Jane does all her own cooking,' Hamish said, more in hope of being contradicted than anything else.

'Not while the hotel is running.' Harriet heated the teapot and spooned in tea-leaves. 'Women come in during the day to do the cleaning and make the beds. But for us, her friends, she does do the cooking.'

'Health stuff?' asked Hamish.

'Well, yes, but you only have to suffer for the next few days. I'm doing a traditional Christmas dinner, and, of course, tonight's dinner.'

'Which is?'

'Very simple. Sirloin steak, baked potato, peas and carrots, salad. Before that, soup; and after that, butterscotch pudding.' She filled the teapot.

'And were you all friends before you met up here?'

'No,' said Harriet. 'We're all new to each other. In fact, I was very surprised to get Jane's invitation. We're not that close. I felt I was putting on too much weight – oh, about four years ago – and went to a health farm in Surrey. Jane was there, slim as ever, but finding out how a health farm was run. We talked a lot and then met once or twice in London for lunch. How did you meet her?'

'I'm a friend o' a friend o' hers,' said Hamish. 'That's all. I had nowhere to go this Christmas and she asked me along.'

The grey eyes regarding him were shrewd. 'And that's all? You're not Jane's latest?'

'Hardly,' said Hamish stiffly, 'with her husband present.'

'Her *ex*-husband. But that wouldn't stop Jane. Anyway, she's made a go of things here. Of course, she imports a lot of staff during the tourist season, chef, masseur, waitresses, the lot. The Todds, that's Heather and Diarmuid, were paying guests, and so they're now here as non-paying friends. The same with the Carpenters.'

'More like acquaintances than friends.'

'Exactly. Off with you. I've got to prepare dinner.' Harriet took down a tray and put teapot, cup and saucer, sugar and milk on it, handed it to Hamish, and shooed him out.

Hamish returned to the lounge, carrying the tray. He was feeling much more cheerful. He liked Harriet Shaw.

But no sooner had he taken off his sports jacket and tie, for the room was hot and there did not seem to be any rigid dress code, and established himself in an armchair, than Heather Todd bore down on him and stood over him, her hands on her hips. 'Are you a Highlander?' she demanded.

'Yes,' said Hamish, carefully pouring tea and determined to enjoy it.

She threw back her head and laughed. It was a copy of that laugh of Jane's, which always sounded as though Jane herself had copied it from someone else.

'A Highlander, and yet you are prepared to contribute to the rape of your country.'

Hamish's eyes travelled up and down her body with calculated insolence. 'Right now, I've never felt less like raping anyone or anything in ma life.'

Heather snorted, and one sandalled foot pawed the carpet. 'What of the Highland clearances?' she demanded.

'That wass the last century.'

'Burning the poor Highlanders' houses over their heads, driving them out of their homes to make way for sheep. And now it's trees!'

'I hivnae heard o' one cottager being turned out to make way for a tree,' said Hamish, trying to peer round her tightly corseted figure to see if Jane or anyone else looked like coming to his rescue.

'What have you to say for yourself?' Heather was asking.

'What I haff to say,' said Hamish, his suddenly sibilant accent betraying his annoyance, 'is that when the Hydro Electric board was burying whole villages under man-made lakes, your sort never breathed a word. Now that it iss politically fashionable to bleat about the environment, it's hard for folks like me to believe you give a damn.'

Heather did not listen to him. He was to learn that once launched, you could say what you liked, she never heard a word. Irritated, he rose and pushed past her and sat on the other side of the room.

He was joined by John Wetherby. 'I could kill that woman,' said John. 'Pontificates from morning till night.'

'Well, maybe her husband will do the job for you.' Hamish looked longingly at the tea he had been forced to abandon.

'Him! That wimp. Have you seen him pass a mirror? He stops dead-still and gazes longingly at himself like a man looking at a lover.'

'Let's talk about something else,' said Hamish. 'What brought you here?'

'I am Jane's ex-husband.'

'Aye, just so, but what brought you?'

'Oh, I get you. I couldn't believe she'd made such a go of things. When we were married, she was always full of hare-brained schemes to make money. That's how I got her to agree to a divorce. I said I would put up the money for this place if she agreed. I thought she would be back after a year, asking me to bail her out, but not a bit of it.'

'And weren't you embarrassed about seeing her again . . . after the divorce, I mean?'

He gave a cackle of laughter. 'You don't know Jane. Have you heard her psycho-babble yet? There's not one idea in that head of hers that doesn't come straight out of a woman's magazine. An article on "How to Be Friends With Your Ex" was one she enjoyed a lot. Are you the latest amour? She occasionally liked a bit of the rough stuff.'

Hamish was too amazed to feel insulted at this bit of blatant snobbery. 'Did she have affairs when you were married?'

'Yes, she said we had become sexually stagnant and went out to experiment.' His voice grew reflective. 'It was that hairy truck-driver I couldn't take.'

Hamish gave John Wetherby a prim look of startled disapproval and rose and moved away. The Carpenters, surely, would be safe company. Sheila was reading a book and Ian was sipping a large whisky and smiling vaguely at nothing.

He sat down next to Ian. 'Topping place,' said Ian, looking around.

'I hear you're a farmer,' said Hamish. 'Funny, I wouldn't have thought farmers would go to health farms. Although, come to think of it, maybe that's not true. I just had a vague idea that perhaps health fanatics went in for it.'

Ian patted his round stomach complacently. 'Sheila keeps up with all the fads. We each lost five pounds when we were here in the summer. Of course, we put it all back on again the week we got home. Didn't we, sweetie?'

'Mmm?' Sheila was buried in a book with a pink cover called *Love's Abiding Passion*. Her lips were moving slightly and she was breathing heavily through her nose.

And then Heather was before them. 'What are you reading, Sheila?' she demanded. Sheila gave a little sigh and held up the book so that Heather could read the title.

'My dear, dear Sheila,' said Heather, shaking her head. 'Surely you can find something better than that pap?'

'It's a marvellous book,' said Sheila, her fat cheeks turning pink.

Heather suddenly snatched it out of Sheila's hand and flicked over the pages and then gleefully read aloud. ' "There was a tearing sound and the thin silk cascaded at her feet. He thrust his hot body against her naked one and she could feel his aroused masculinity bulging against her thigh." I ask you, Sheila, how can you bear to read a book like that?'

Sheila snatched it back and heaved herself out of the sofa and waddled from the room. Her husband stood up and glared at Heather. 'It's better than the works of Marx any day.'

'It would considerably improve your wife's mind to read Karl Marx.'

'Yah!' said Ian. 'What d'you lot think about the fall of Communism in Eastern Europe, hey?'

'That was not real Communism,' said Heather. 'Real Communism . . .'

'Stuff it, you old crow,' said the farmer and left the room with the same waddling walk as his wife. Hamish felt like running after him and shaking his hand.

Before Heather could speak to him again, he darted for the door and let himself out into the night. The high wind of earlier in the day had descended to ground level and was tearing and shrieking and moaning along the shore, where seals lay at the edge of the crashing waves, their curious eyes gleaming pink from the neon sign of The Happy Wanderer.

The wind was cold. Hamish wished he had remembered to put on his jacket. Priscilla often called him a moocher. He hugged his thin body against the bite of the wind. He should have stayed where he was in Lochdubh. He could imagine someone saying they would like to strangle Jane, but no-one would really think of doing it. There was not enough real about the woman to encourage great love or great hate. And that marriage of hers! When John had been talking about that truck driver, Hamish had felt slightly sick.

His cold would get worse if he stayed outside. He walked back in. Jane was standing talking to Heather. Heather was not hectoring Jane about anything but looking at her with open-mouthed admiration and hanging on every word.

'Is there a telephone?' Hamish asked Jane.

'There's one in my office you can use. It's over there,' said Jane, pointing to a door on the right of the lounge.

Hamish walked over to where she had pointed. A ceramic sign on the door said 'Jane's Office' and was decorated by a wreath of painted wild flowers.

The office was strictly functional; large steel desk, steel filing cabinets, two easy chairs for visitors.

Hamish sat behind the desk, picked up the phone and dialled Tommel Castle, now called Tommel Castle Hotel. He recognized the voice of Mary Anderson, a local girl, who operated the hotel switchboard. 'Can I speak to Priscilla?' he asked.

'Herself is not back,' said Mary. 'She went to Rogart.'

'Is the storm bad?' asked Hamish, trying to blot out pictures of a car upended in a blizzard by the side of the road with a woman and a dog lying beside it.

'Oh, it's real bad. That's Hamish, isn't it?'

'Yes. Has she phoned?'

'No, but they got it worse over there than here, so folks are saying. Maybe the lines are down.'

Hamish thanked her, put down the receiver, then lifted it again and dialled his parents' home.

His mother answered. 'Is Priscilla there?' demanded Hamish, his voice sharp with anxiety.

'Aye, she's here. But you cannae talk to her, son.'

'Why?'

'The poor lassie's still fast asleep by the fire. My, Hamish, she used to be the most beautiful girl I've ever seen, and now she's nothing but skin and bone. She cannae leave. She'll need to stay the night. I'll let her sleep a bit and then give her a good supper and put her to bed.'

'Have you the room?'

'Och, yes, we'll put a cot bed in the girls' room. How's yourself?'

'I'm just fine.'

'Is it a grand place?'

'Well, it's a health farm, sort of mock-Spanish villa.'

'On Eileencraig! My, my.'

'Dinner,' called Jane, putting her head round the door.

'I've got to go, Ma,' said Hamish quickly. 'I'll phone tomorrow.'

He said goodbye and sat for a moment looking at the phone. What on earth would the elegant and fastidious Priscilla make of his noisy, easygoing family?

He rose then and went out through the lounge to the dining-room. It was panelled in pine wood. Several small tables had been put together to make a big one and it was covered by a red-and-white-checked cloth and decorated with candles in wine bottles. A stag's head ornamented one wall, and Hamish noticed to his surprise that it was fake. He hadn't known that such a thing existed. Jane probably did not approve of bits of real animal being used, hence the fake head and the synthetic skins on the lounge floor.

Dinner was excellent and Hamish could only be glad that he was seated between the Carpenters and therefore protected by their bulk from Heather. Also, to his relief, conversation at dinner was innocuous. Jane was explaining that they would all go for a walk along the shore in the morning and then, after lunch, take a walk inland while there was still some light. Hamish enjoyed the excellent meal washed down with some good claret. He began to feel mellow. It was not going to be such a disaster after all. But he should show some gesture toward earning his keep.

As soon as dinner was over, he asked Jane to show him that bathroom heater.

Jane let him into her bedroom, through a door emblazoned with the legend 'Sir Walter Scott.' It was furnished pretty much the same as the one allotted to Hamish, except that there were two bookshelves stuffed with women's magazines instead of one.

He went into the bathroom and examined the heater carefully and then stood back and looked at the ceiling.

There was a patch of damp and black mould beginning to form on it. He was sure the builder had been right and that the heater had fallen off the wall because of the damp. In fact, probably the whole structure of the health farm needed to be treated for damp, but to tell Jane that at this early date would make him feel more of a fraud than he was and so he murmured non-committally that he would take another look at it on the following day, and that he would probably start his investigations by going to see Mrs Bannerman.

Jane stood very close beside him. 'I see what Priscilla means,' she said. 'You *are* very competent.'

Hamish shied and took a nervous step back.

'How did you meet Priscilla?' he asked.

'It was at a party in London,' replied Jane. 'Such a boring party, we decided to leave early and went to a bar for a drink and got talking. We had a few lunches after that.'

'And when did you last see her?'

'About three years ago, and then I heard this summer that her father had gone bust and turned the castle into an hotel.'

Hardly a friendship, thought Hamish. 'Shall we join the others?' he said, easing around her and making for the door.

Jane looked a little disappointed but followed him out. 'Pity,' she murmured. 'I've never had a policeman before.' Or rather, that's what Hamish thought she'd said.

The rest of the guests were back in the television lounge and grouped around the set. It was a talk show. A famous film star told everyone how he had got off the booze, and he was followed by a famous romantic novelist.

Heather's eyes narrowed. 'Just look at that silly woman. It gars me grue to see creatures like that making all that money producing rubbish.'

Sheila flushed and Hamish noticed that she slid

the romance she had been holding on her lap down the side of the chair.

'Here, wait a minute,' said Harriet crossly. 'I may only write cookery books, but I do know something about romance writers. To be successful you can't write down, and very few of them make big money.'

Heather sniffed. 'Money for old rope, if you ask me. And the historical ones are the worst. I doubt if they even open a history book.'

'Well, it's the romance that sells it, not the historical content,' said Harriet soothingly. 'For example, if I wrote a book about the French Revolution, I would describe the tyranny and horror and how the storming of the Bastille was only to get at the arsenal. There were only seven people freed, you know. Now your true romance writer would see it more through the eyes of Hollywood. Thousands of prisoners would be released while the heroine, dressed in rags, led the liberators. Great stuff. I really sometimes wonder if the less romance writers know, the better.

'Or, for example, I would describe a shiekh of the desert as a fat little man with glasses and a dish-towel on his head. Your true romance writer would have a hawk-eyed Rudolph Valentino character in Turkish turban and thigh-boots. It's a harmless escape.'

'Harmless!' Heather snorted. 'It's even got women like poor Sheila here stuffing her mind with rubbish.'

'For heaven's sake,' said Harriet crossly, 'you watch the most awful pap on television, day and night. There was a programme on Channel Four last night about some Hollywood producer who does soft-porn horror films and who was treated by the interviewer as a serious intellectual. Anyone who writes popular literature, on the other hand, is treated like a charlatan, and do you know why, Heather? It's because the world is full of morons who think they could write a book if only they had the time. You're just jealous!'

'Yes, if you're so bloody superior,' said John Wetherby, 'why don't *you* write a book, Heather?'

Heather looked at them like a baffled bull. Hamish guessed it was the very first time during her visit to the island that she had been under attack.

'Aren't we all getting *cross*?' cried Jane. 'Switch the goggle box off, John, and we'll all have a game of Monopoly instead.'

Hamish was then able to see another side to Jane, the good-business/hostess side. She flattered Heather by asking her questions about the latest shows in Glasgow as she led them through to the lounge and spread out the Monopoly board on the table. She teased Sheila charmingly on having such a devoted husband and said she ought to write an article and tell everyone her secret. She congratulated Harriet on a beautiful meal and told Diarmuid, Heather's husband, that he was so good-looking she was going to take some photographs of him to use on the health-farm brochure.

They all settled down in a better humour to a

long game of Monopoly and nobody seemed to mind very much when Heather won.

Hamish at last went off to bed. The bed was comfortable and the central heating excellent. He wondered why Jane had seen fit to have extra wall heaters put in all the bathrooms, and then reflected that she was a clever enough business woman to cosset her guests by seeming to supply them with a rigorous regime of exercise outside while pampering them with warmth and comfort indoors.

He was sure no-one was trying to kill her. And yet, he could not shake off a nagging feeling of uneasiness. He put it down, after some thought, to the fact that he disliked Heather intensely and had been shocked by John's revelations about his marriage. He would avoid them as much as possible. Harriet Shaw, now, was worth spending time with, and on that comfortable thought he drifted off to sleep.

Sheila Carpenter sat in front of the dressing-table in the room called Mary of Argyll which she shared with her husband. She wound rollers in her hair while her husband lay in bed, watching her.

'I could kill her,' said Sheila suddenly.

'Who?'

'Heather, of course.'

'I'll do it for you, pet. Don't let her bother you. She's not worth it.'

'Petty, stupid snob,' said Sheila with uncharacteristic viciousness.

*   *   *

'Who is that long drip of a Highlander?' demanded John Wetherby. Jane shrugged. She was putting away the Monopoly pieces in their box. 'Just some friend of Priscilla's.'

'You can't fool me. For your benefit, your dear friend Heather told me this Macbeth was your latest.'

'It's not true,' said Jane. 'And Heather would not say anything malicious like that.'

'Oh, no? She's a first-class bitch and I feel like bashing her head in.'

Jane studied him seriously and then said in a voice of patient reason, 'You must stop this irrational jealousy, John. It's not flattering or even sexually motivated. It is simply based on totally irrational masculine possessiveness. It said in an article I was reading the other day . . .'

'Pah!' shouted John and stomped off to his room.

Diarmuid Todd sat at the dressing-table and trimmed his fingernails. His wife, Heather, was reading *The Oppression of the Working Classes in a Capitalist Society*. She read as far as page 2 and then put the book down. 'What do you think of our Jane's latest?'

Diarmuid paused, and then continued working on his nails with all the single-minded fastidiousness of a cat at its toilet. 'Who do you mean?' he asked.

'Why, that Highland chap, Hamish something-or-another.'

Her husband put away the scissors in his leather

manicure case and then took out an orangewood stick and began to clean his nails. 'I don't think he's anything other than a friend, Heather, and I hope you haven't been going around saying anything else.'

His usually bland Scottish voice had a slight edge to it. 'Maybe not,' said Heather. 'Jane's a very attractive-looking woman but hardly a man-eater. There's something, well, sexless about her.'

She patted the springy waves of her permanently waved hair with a complacent hand before picking up her book again.

The stick snapped in Diarmuid's suddenly tensed fingers and he threw his wife a look of pure and unadulterated hatred.

Harriet Shaw creamed her face vigorously and then slapped at what she feared might become a double chin one of these days and wished she had not come. The Carpenters were sweet, but Heather was too much to take. Thank goodness for that Hamish fellow. He was charming and quite attractive in a way with his fiery-red hair and hazel eyes. Better stick with him till the holiday was over or she would end up killing Heather. She amused herself before falling asleep by thinking out ways to get rid of Heather and then how to dispose of the body, until, with a smile on her lips, she fell fast asleep.

CHAPTER THREE

Though by whim, envy, or resentment led,
They damn those authors whom they never read.
—CHARLES CHURCHILL

To Hamish's surprise, breakfast, cooked by Jane, turned out to be an excellent meal, although he missed not having any tea or coffee. It consisted of toast and low-cholesterol margarine, fresh grapefruit, muesli, and a large glass of freshly squeezed orange juice.

The breakfast was marred only by the seething emotions around him. Jane had appeared wearing pink denim shorts with a bib front over a white-and-pink-checked blouse and walking boots in tan leather. She was shortly followed by Heather, wearing exactly the same outfit.

Heather's face was flushed and angry and Diarmuid looked sulky. They had just had a row. The normally placid Diarmuid had suddenly snapped that if Heather thought Jane sexless, then why did she try to dress like her? It only made her look like a fright. And certainly Heather did look awful, having rolls and bumps of flesh where Jane had none, and fat white hairy legs, Heather believing that to shave one's legs was merely pandering to masculine sexism. Jane looked at Heather as she entered and something for a moment glittered in the depths of her eyes and then was gone.

Sheila had carried her romance to the breakfast table and was reading it, occasionally darting nasty little looks at Heather, and her husband also darted angry little looks at Heather, so that the round Carpenters looked more like twins than husband and wife.

John Wetherby was glowering at his breakfast. He was wearing a V-necked pullover over a blue shirt and a tightly knotted tie, grey flannels, and walking shoes, his idea of suitable wear for a hiker.

Jane rose and addressed them at the end of the meal. 'This will not do,' she said gaily. 'There is a nasty atmosphere and we should all be having a lovely, lovely time.' She lifted a box and put it on the table. 'I have here a supply of balloons, thread, and pencil and paper. Now, I suggest we each write down our resentments, blow up our balloons, and carry them outside and watch them all float away!'

'Oh, for God's sake, Jane,' snapped her ex-husband. 'Be your age.'

'Don't be stuffy,' said Heather, 'Sounds like fun. Come on, Sheila, get your head out of that trash.' She gave that laugh copied from Jane. 'It's like watching a rather nice little pig with its head in the trough.'

'Watch your mouth, you rotten bitch,' shouted Ian.

'I know what it is,' cried Jane, holding up her hands. 'We need some fresh air to blow the cobwebs away. Forget about the balloons. Where's your Christmas spirit? Get your coats and *off* we go.'

They all meekly rose to their feet. 'I don't think I can bear this,' said Harriet to Hamish.

He smiled down at her. 'I have to go over to the village this morning, and maybe there's a bar there . . .'

'I'll come with you,' said Harriet. 'Don't tell the others. We'll just join the end of the crocodile and then veer off.'

Jane set out at the head of the group. Her voice floated back to them. 'Let's sing! All together now. "One man went to mow . . ." '

'Come on,' said Hamish to Harriet as the group straggled along the beach behind Jane.

The air was warmer than the day before, but a howling gale was still blowing. Snatches of Jane's singing reached the ears of Hamish and Harriet as they made their way inland and on to the road that led to the village. The rising sun was low on the horizon, curlews piped dismally from the heather, and sea-gulls crouched on the ground, occasionally taking off to battle with the gale.

They tried to talk but at last fell silent, for the shrieking wind meant they had to shout. Harriet was wearing a tweed jacket and matching skirt. Her short brown hair streaked with grey was crisp and curly. She walked with an easy stride by Hamish's side. Hamish was happy. The silence between them was companionable, tinged with a conspiratorial edge prompted by their escape from the others.

They turned a bend in the road and in front of them stood a very battered old Fiat truck, parked in the middle. They made their way around it and stopped short. A small man was sitting at the side of the road in front of the truck, weeping bitterly.

'Hey,' cried Hamish, crouching down beside the forlorn figure. 'What's your trouble?'

'It iss him,' said the man, raising a tear-stained face and jerking a gnarled thumb in the direction of the truck. 'He iss out to kill me.'

Hamish got up, and motioning Harriet to stand well back, he went quickly to the truck. There was no-one in the cabin and nothing in the back but barrels of lobster.

He loped back and sat down on the road beside the man and said coaxingly, 'Now, then, there's no-one there. Who are you talking about?'

'Him!' said the little man passionately, and again that thumb jerked at the truck. 'Can't you see him, sitting there, watching me?'

The truck-driver was probably only in his forties, but hard weather and a hard life made him appear older. Like most of the islanders, he was small in stature. He had a weather-beaten face. Sparse grey hairs clung to his brown scalp.

Harriet bent down and shouted above the tumult of the wind, 'But there is not a soul about except for us.'

'Wait a bit.' Hamish held up his hand. 'Do you mean the *truck* is trying to kill you?'

'Aye, the beast! The beast. Wass I not loading the lobsters and did he not back into me and try for to tip me into the sea?'

'And did you not have the brakes on?' said Hamish cynically. 'What is your name?'

'Geordie Mason.'

'Well, listen, Geordie, stop your havering. I am Hamish Macbeth, and this is Harriet Shaw. We're going into Skulag. I'll hae a look at your truck and drive it for ye.'

Geordie rubbed his eyes with his sleeve. 'Wid ye dae that? Himself will no' mind. It's jist me he cannae thole.'

Hamish drew Harriet aside. 'It'll save us a walk,' he said. 'I'm sure the wee man is harmless. Probably been at the methylated spirits.'

Hamish climbed into the driving-seat, Geordie sat next to him, and Harriet on the other side. It was an old-fashioned bench seat, and so it could take the three of them comfortably.

Hamish turned the key in the ignition. The engine gave a cough and remained silent. 'Ye've got to tell himself it's no' me that's driving.' Geordie had recovered from his grief and seemed almost proud of demonstrating the bloody-mindedness of his vehicle.

Harriet stifled a giggle. 'All right,' said Hamish amiably. 'Does he have a name?'

'He's an agent o' the deil, no' a pet.'

'Why he?' asked Harriet. 'I mean boats and

planes and things like that are she.'

'I jist ken,' said Geordie, folding his arms and glaring through the windscreen.

'Oh, Fiat truck,' said Hamish Macbeth, 'this is your friend speaking. This is not your master, Geordie Mason. We're going to Skulag, so be a nice truck and get a move on.'

He grinned as he turned the key in the ignition, a grin that faded as the old engine roared into life.

'Told ye so, but would yis listen?' demanded Geordie with gloomy satisfaction.

Hamish drove steadily down the road, reflecting that he should be taking better care of Harriet. Perhaps Geordie would start seeing green snakes or spiders before they reached the village. And yet the man did not smell of drink.

'Is there a pub of some kind?' he asked.

'Aye,' said Geordie. 'Down at the hotel, The Highland Comfort, next tae the jetty.'

The village of Skulag was a small cluster of low houses standing end-on to the sea, some of them thatched in the old manner with heather. There was no-one to be seen as they rattled down the cobbled main street. Hamish parked neatly in front of the hotel, which was on a small rise above the jetty. It was a two-storeyed white-washed building, originally built in the Victorian era as a holiday home for some misguided Glasgow merchant who had survived only one holiday summer before putting the place up for sale. It had been an hotel ever since.

Inside, apart from a hutch of a reception desk,

the rooms leading off the hall still bore their Victorian legends of 'Drawing-Room', 'Smoking-Room,' and 'Billiard-Room.'

Hamish, who had been in such hotels before, opened the door marked 'Drawing-Room' and there, sure enough, was the bar along one wall. Along the other wall was a line of glass-and-steel windows overlooking the jetty.

'What are you having?' asked Hamish. 'I'd sit at a table over at the window, Harriet. I doubt if the natives are friendly.' He nodded towards the line of small men in caps who were propping up the bar. They looked back at him with sullen hostility.

'A whisky and water,' said Harriet.

Hamish ordered two whiskies and water and then carried them over to a table at the window.

'There's that poor mad truck-driver,' said Harriet.

Hamish looked out. The truck was where he'd left it, parked on the rise. A little below, at the entrance to the jetty, stood Geordie, leaning forward against the force of the wind and trying to light a cigarette.

And then, in front of Hamish's horrified eyes, the truck began to creep forward and Geordie was standing in a direct line of its approach.

Hamish struggled with the rusty catch of the window and swung it open. 'Geordie!' he yelled desperately. 'Look out!'

Geordie looked up, startled. The truck stopped dead.

'Wait a minute,' said Hamish to Harriet.

He ran outside the hotel and straight up to Geordie. 'You'd better have the brakes on that truck of yours checked,' he shouted against the screaming of the wind.

Geordie shrugged. 'What's the point? Anyway, himself stopped when he heard you.'

Hamish went back to the truck and climbed inside the cabin. The keys were still in the ignition. He switched on the engine and put his foot gently on the accelerator. Nothing happened. The brakes held firm.

He switched off the engine and got down and walked to the front of the truck. There was no explanation why the thing had suddenly stopped. It was parked on a slope, it had started moving, and it had stopped when he called.

He shrugged and went back into the bar to join Harriet.

'Odd,' he said. 'Did you see that?'

'He should get it checked,' said Harriet. 'A good mechanic would sort the trouble out in no time.'

The men at the bar were staring at both of them and talking rapidly in Gaelic. 'What are they saying?' asked Harriet.

'My Gaelic's a bit rusty,' said Hamish, 'but they are saying, I gather, some pretty nasty things about Jane. That wee man there with the black hair is saying she should be driven off the island and the other one is saying someone should kill the bitch.'

'How awful! Why are they so nasty about her? Jane's harmless.'

'I think it's just because they are nasty people,'

said Hamish. He shouted something in Gaelic in a sharp voice and the men relapsed into sulky silence.

The door to the bar opened and a large policeman lumbered in. He had a huge round fiery-red face and small watery eyes. Those eyes rested briefly on Hamish and then sharpened. He marched up to their table.

'Whit are you doing here?' Harriet looked from Hamish to the policeman in surprise.

'Holiday, Sandy,' said Hamish briefly.

'At The Happy Wanderer?'

Hamish nodded.

'You need to pit on weight, man, no' lose it.' Sandy looked cynically down at Hamish's thin and lanky form. 'Wait a minute. The place is closed. She's got her friends there.'

'One of which is me,' said Hamish equably.

'You're up tae something.' Sandy looked mulish. 'And if I find you're poaching on my territory, I'll phone Strathbane and have ye sent home.'

'Do that.' Hamish gazed up at him blandly.

Sandy muttered something, turned and threw a longing look at the bar, and then slouched out.

'What was all that about?' asked Harriet. 'Have you a criminal record?'

Hamish shook his head. 'I'll tell you the truth if you promise to keep it to yourself. I am the local copper in a village called Lochdubh on the west coast of Sutherland. Jane asked me to come because she was afraid someone was trying to kill her.'

'Oh, the bathroom heater. But that was an

accident. But of course I won't tell anyone who you are.'

'Jane herself thought it an accident but she went to a Mrs Bannerman in this village and got her fortune told. This Mrs Bannerman told her that someone from far away was trying to kill her. Jane had also just missed being hit by a falling rock. She was worried it might be one of you. I plan to see Mrs Bannerman this morning. Would you like to come along?'

Harriet grinned. 'Lead on, Sherlock. This is all very exciting.'

'Now that you know the truth about me,' said Hamish, 'tell me what you think of the other guests. Let's start with the horrible Heather.'

'I've met types like Heather on visits to Glasgow,' said Harriet. 'She seems to spend an awful lot on entertaining any visiting celebrity she can, running a sort of Glaswegian salon. She's a fairly rich, old-fashioned Communist, looking for another totalitarian regime to worship now that Stalinism has been finally discredited. Says she was brought up in the Gorbals when it was a really horrible slum and tells very colourful stories and I am not sure I believe any of them. Quotes Sartre in very bad French. Refers to celebrities by their first names, Rudi being Rudolph Nureyev, things like that. Adores Jane and is jealous of her at the same time. Jane has no political affiliations that I know of, but she hails from an old county family, and that's enough for a snob like Heather. Jane's maiden name is Bellingham. Her pa owns a minor stately home in Wiltshire and Heather keeps hinting she'd like an invitation. Heather is the kind who hangs around the private section of stately homes on view to the public in the hope that one of the family will emerge and recognize one of their own kind.'

'I don't get it,' said Hamish. 'And her a Communist!'

'When it comes to social climbing, such as Heather never lets politics get in the way, hence her friendship with Jane. Hates romance writers. There's still plenty of first-class romance writers around, but she reserves her venom for what used to be called novelettes, you know, the laird and the country girl, or the advertising exec and the secretary. It's still the laird and the country girl or whatever, but with lashings of sex thrown in. Nothing too vulgar. Lots of euphemisms. She says all their royalties should be taken from them by the government and given to writers' workshops to help the up and coming intellectual. She's about fifty-three. I would say Diarmuid is a bit younger.

'I don't think there's much more to Diarmuid than what you see. He is a supremely vain man and yet appears proud of his unlikeable wife. That atmosphere between them this morning was totally new. He's in real estate, so he can't be doing too well at the moment with the fall in the market.

'John Wetherby. Well, that seems to have been an odd marriage. He delights in running Jane down. I sometimes wonder if she had affairs to score off him. I sometimes wonder if she had any affairs at all. She is a good business woman, but I can't seem to find anything deeper than what you see on the surface. John is a successful barrister, opinionated to the point of smugness. Why he accepted Jane's invitation I do not know. I cannot see one trace of affection in his manner towards her. I gather he is a trifle mean and Jane told me he probably jumped at the idea of a free holiday.'

Hamish winced and said quickly, 'And the Carpenters?'

'He's got a farm in north Yorkshire. At first when I saw them flirting with each other and cooing at each other, I thought that marriage looked too good to be true, but I think they are a genuinely nice and rather innocent couple.'

'And Harriet Shaw?'

She smiled and he liked the way her eyes crinkled up. 'Widow, no children, writes cookery books which are moderately successful. Gets money from occasional television programmes and cookery articles for magazines. Wonders what she is doing on this bleak island talking about suspects to a policeman.'

Hamish laughed. 'Drink up and let's see this Bannerman woman. I'll just find out at the bar where she lives.'

Harriet waited for him at the door. 'Last cottage at the end of the main street, on the left,' said Hamish, returning from the bar. 'Let's get out of here. You could cut the hostility with a knife.'

As they were leaving, a housemaid, about to descend the stairs, saw them, and retreated quickly.

'Nobody loves us,' mourned Hamish.

They walked down the main street, and women appeared outside their cottages and stood watching them. One approached them, a small woman with a fat white face. She caught hold of Hamish's sleeve and began to talk to him urgently in Gaelic. Hamish listened patiently and then shook himself free and walked on.

'What did she say?' asked Harriet.

'She said that Jane's a whore. There was a bad storm the other week and two of the fishermen were washed overboard. They say it's God's punishment for having a scarlet woman on the island. Jane's been here for two years now. Doesn't she notice any of this? She got me here to protect her because she thinks someone's trying to kill her. Well, after listening to that woman, I've decided that maybe someone is, and if she doesn't shut up shop soon and leave, they'll drown her.'

'How did she know who we are?'

'They saw me arriving with her off the boat. Two men left the bar while we were there. The fact that I spoke to them in Gaelic would go round the village in minutes. Here's this Bannerman woman's place.'

She opened the door before they could knock. 'I knew you wass coming,' she intoned. Harriet looked startled, but Hamish grinned and said, 'Phoned you from the bar, did they?'

'Come in,' she said rather huffily. They entered a low, dark parlour. Mrs Bannerman ushered them into chairs and sat facing them.

She was in her thirties, guessed Hamish, and was wearing what looked like a 1960s Carnaby Street outfit: peasant blouse, flowered skirt, bare feet, and beads. Her hair was long and straggly and she had a thin, unhealthy-looking face and small black eyes. He saw with surprise that her neck was dirty. It was not often one saw a dirty neck these days.

She leaned forward and looked into Hamish's eyes. 'Well, Hamish Macbeth,' she crooned, 'and what haff you to say to me?'

Harriet started, thinking the woman really had psychic powers, but Hamish glanced at the phone in the corner of the room. His conversation with Sandy would have been overheard. Sandy had a loud voice. Sandy had probably dived into the bar after they left and the barman had phoned Mrs Bannerman with the details.

'I am here on holiday,' said Hamish, 'but I would still like to know why you told Mrs Wetherby that someone was trying to kill her or going to kill her.'

'I saw death,' moaned Mrs Bannerman, 'right there at the bottom of the cup. I felt a great blackness come ower me.'

'I think you were put up to it, that's what I think,' said Hamish, becoming tired of all this mumbo-jumbo, particularly as he sensed that Mrs Bannerman was enjoying herself hugely. 'And where is Mr Bannerman?'

'Dead and gone,' she wailed.

'Dead of what?'

'Died innis bed,' she snapped, her voice momentarily coarsening and losing its Highland accent.

'Where?'

'Ah'm I bein' accused o' anything?' demanded Mrs Bannerman angrily.

'Only that I think you're a fraud.'

'Whit?' She rose to her feet in a rage. 'Get oot o' ma hoose and go and bile yer heid!'

'That didn't get you very far,' said Harriet once they were outside.

The Fiat truck rattled along the main street and came to a stop in front of them. 'If you're going back, I'll gie ye a lift,' called Geordie.

'May as well,' said Hamish. They climbed into the cabin.

'Going all right now?' asked Hamish.

'Aye,' said Geordie, 'I gave him a wee bit o' oil, not that he needs it, but he aye likes a treat.'

Hamish stifled a groan. 'Tell me about Mrs Bannerman,' he said. 'She's not an islander, is she?'

'Naw, herself's frae Glasgow. Come up here, must hae been about five years ago.'

'So why all the hostility to Mrs Wetherby and none to her?'

'She doesnae go around dressed in them short skirts,' said Geordie. 'Besides, she knows her tea-leaves and ye go careful wi' someone like that.'

'Did that silly woman tell you that your truck was trying to kill you?' asked Hamish.

'Don't be daft,' said Geordie. 'The truck telt me.'

Hamish gave him an uneasy look, wondering just how deranged Geordie was.

'And what of Mrs Bannerman's husband?'

'Doing a stretch for g.b.h. in Barlinnie Prison.'

68

'What's g.b.h.?' asked Harriet.

'Grievous bodily harm,' said Hamish but with his eyes still fixed curiously on the driver. 'How did you find that out?'

'Her mither arrived frae Glasgow last year on a visit. Rare gossip that woman wass.'

'And who did Bannerman attack?' pursued Hamish.

'I don't know,' said Geordie. 'Will ye leave me tae drive himself in peace?'

They travelled the rest of the way in silence, thanked Geordie when they got off at The Happy Wanderer, and went inside to find the others quite resentful that they had decided to go off on their own.

Hamish asked Jane if he might use her phone and then went into the office and phoned his mother. 'Priscilla gone?' he asked.

'No,' said his mother. 'She can't really travel. The roads are still bad. She started fretting about her father and the guests, so I told her to get on to Mr Johnson at the Lochdubh Hotel. They're closed down for the winter. I told her to ask him to go up and offer his services for the Christmas period and ask a high price. The colonel will want his money's worth out o' Johnson, but he'll respect someone he's paying a lot for.'

'Good idea. But I'll bet she won't do it.'

'She already has,' said his mother triumphantly.

'My! Can I speak to her?'

'No, son, she's out sledging with the children.'

They talked for a little and then Hamish rang

off, trying to imagine Priscilla sledging with his brothers and sisters. Hamish had been an only child for many years, and then, when his mother was in her forties, she had begun to produce brothers and sisters for him, three boys and three girls. This largely explained Hamish's unmarried state, for it was a Highland tradition that the eldest should stay unmarried and help to support the family. He sent everything he could home and had learned to be thrifty, as well as expert at cadging free meals.

Lunch was an edgy affair. He wondered what on earth was up when he entered the dining-room and felt the weight of the silence. Harriet told him afterwards, as they all set out for the afternoon walk with Jane, that Sheila had decided to carry her lunch into the television room in order to watch the midday showing of the Australian soaps. Heather had lectured her on the stupidity of this pastime and had even gone in and switched off the television. Sheila had burst into tears and thrown her first course of vegetable soup at Heather's head.

They marched inland, Jane striding out in front, the rest trailing behind. The sky was darkening above and the sun was sinking low on the horizon and then, just before darkness fell, Jane stopped and pointed to the west. It was an awesome sight. They were almost at the centre of the island. It was below sea-level. Out to the west, it looked as if the whole of the Atlantic were about to come charging down on them. 'How terrifying to look *up* at the sea,' said Harriet. She moved closer to Hamish and he put an arm around her shoulders and she leaned against him briefly, then straightened up and disengaged herself, her cheeks pink.

The exercise had revived everyone's spirits and there was a sort of silent agreement not to quarrel. John Wetherby caught up with Jane and they headed back to the hotel. Hamish noticed that John and Jane were talking like old friends.

Dinner was pleasant. Then television destroyed everything. Heather wanted to watch a production of *King Lear* in modern dress; the rest wanted to watch 'Cheers' and 'The Golden Girls.' Heather lectured them bitterly on the folly of watching rubbish produced by American imperalists. Jane put it to a vote and the American imperialists won. Heather stalked off to bed.

Immediately the atmosphere lightened. Diarmuid stayed to watch the comedies and laughed as hard as the rest. But when it was over, John Wetherby suddenly glared at his ex-wife, who was sharing a sofa with Diarmuid. Jane had changed into a short miniskirt and blouse. 'Pull your skirt down, for God's sake,' he snapped. 'You're showing everything.'

Jane blushed furiously. It was the first time Hamish had seen her really put out. Then she gave that merry laugh and suggested they all move through to the lounge for drinks.

Hamish retired to bed early. Once more he felt gloomy. Once more he wished he had never come.

* * *

The next day was a hell of low cloud and driving rain. House-bound, the guests idled about. Hamish began to read some of Jane's magazines to pass the time. He found a serial in *Women's Home Journal* that was extremely good and rifled through the back numbers until he had got the whole book and settled down comfortably to read.

'I'm going out for a walk,' called Jane. 'Anyone coming?'

Diarmuid half-started to his feet but his wife pulled him back down. No-one else moved.

'Then I'll go myself,' said Jane. She was wearing a bright-yellow oilskin. She hesitated at the door and looked at John Wetherby. He grunted and picked up his newspaper and hid behind it.

Jane walked out.

The day dragged past. But at four in the afternoon, Hamish realized it was pitch-black outside and Jane had not returned.

'Where's Jane?' he asked suddenly.

'Probably in the kitchen,' said John. He was now playing chess with Diarmuid.

'I'll look,' said Harriet quickly.

She came back after about ten minutes. 'She's not in her room, and not in the kitchen, not anywhere. Her oilskin's missing.'

Hamish got his own coat and made for the door. 'Wait a bit,' called Harriet. 'I'm coming with you.'

They collected torches from a ledge beside the door and made their way out into the howling gale. 'Where would she go?' shouted Hamish.

'The beach,' said Harriet. 'She usually walks on the beach when she's on her own.'

They walked rapidly along the beach. The tide was coming in and great waves fanned out at their feet. Hamish was cursing himself. He had taken his duties too lightly. He should never have let her go off on her own. 'You'd better take my hand,' he shouted at Harriet. 'I don't want you getting lost as well.'

Harriet had a warm, dry hand. Despite his anxiety, Hamish enjoyed the feel of it.

And then the wind dropped, just like that, as it sometimes does on the islands, with dramatic suddenness. There was no sound but the crashing of the waves.

They stopped and listened hard.

Harriet squeezed his hand urgently. 'Listen! I heard something. A faint cry.'

'Probably a sheep.'

'Shhh!'

In the pause between one wave and the next, Hamish heard a faint call. It was coming from someplace in front of them. It could be a nocturnal sea-bird, but it had to be investigated. They walked slowly on, stopping and listening.

And then they heard it, a cry for help. Hamish swung the torch around and its powerful beam picked out a pillbox on a bluff above the beach, one of those pillboxes built out of concrete during the Second World War. Dragging Harriet after him, he ran towards it. 'Jane!' he called.

'Here!' came the faint reply.

A door had been put on the pillbox, quite a modern door with a shining new bolt. Hamish jerked back the bolt and Jane Wetherby tumbled out. As Harriet comforted her, he shone the torch inside. It was full of old barrels and fishing nets and bits of machinery. Someone was using it as a storehouse.

He went back to Jane. 'What happened?' he asked.

'I was walking along the beach and I saw the pillbox door open. It was the first time I had seen it open. It was a bit nosy of me, but I went to have a look inside. Nothing but nets and things. And then someone pushed me and I went flying inside and the door was slammed and bolted behind me. Those village children, no doubt.'

'Are you all right?' asked Harriet anxiously.

'Yes, fine. I wasn't scared. I just didn't want to spend the night in there. It was getting so cold.'

The night *was* bitter cold. Hamish walked back, worried. A less healthy and robust woman than Jane, locked up there and left for, say, twenty-four hours before she was found, might have died of exposure. 'Who owns that pillbox, or rather, who uses it?' he asked.

'I don't know,' said Jane.

Back at the health farm, and after Jane had answered all the guests' questions, Hamish took her aside and said it was time he had a quiet talk with her, perhaps when the others had retired for the night.

'Come to my room,' said Jane.

Hamish eyed her nervously and scratched his red hair. 'What about the kitchen?' he suggested, and Jane agreed. Twelve o'clock was decided on.

The guests retired early. Hamish lay reading more magazines until midnight. Then he left his room and went through to the kitchen. He pushed open the door.

Jane was standing by the table in the centre of the room. She was wearing a black, transparent nightie over a suspender belt and black stockings and very high-heeled black shoes. 'Good evening, copper,' she said.

CHAPTER FOUR

And sadly reflecting,
That a lover forsaken
A new love may get,
But a neck when once broken
Can never be set.
—WILLIAM WALSH

Hamish stood in the doorway, his eyes averted. 'I'll chust wait here, Jane, while you go and put something on.'

'Oh, come *on*, Hamish,' she said breathily, and moved towards him.

'I'll wait for you in the lounge,' said Hamish crossly. 'Don't you dare come near me until you make yourself decent.' And he stalked off, as stiffly as a cat.

Jane appeared in the lounge five minutes later. She had put on a housecoat that covered her from throat to heel. 'Better?' she queried, tossing her hair.

'Much better,' said Hamish, 'Now, lassie, chust you sit yerself down and tell me what on earth you were playing at.'

'Hamish Macbeth, I shouldn't need to spell it out for you. A bit of fun.'

He shook his head in amazement. 'That's hardly the way to go about it. What would you have felt like in the morning?'

'Much better,' said Jane earnestly. 'Sexual intercourse is a very healthy exercise and good for the skin.'

'So's jogging. Jane, Jane, have you no feelings at all? Do you never feel rejection when a pass is turned down, shame when it isn't?'

Jane looked at him in a puzzled way, one finger to her brow. Then her face cleared. 'Calvinism. That's it!' she cried. 'You have been brought up to have your mind warped by repressive religion.'

'And you haff been brought up to have your mind warped by women's magazines. I thought all this free love was out of fashion anyway,' said Hamish wearily. 'We're not getting anywhere. I must tell you flat that when John told me about your affairs, I felt sick.'

'Which one in particular?' asked Jane curiously.

'Some truck-driver.'

'Oh, that. The fellow was as queer as a coot. I only brought him around to annoy John.'

'Why?'

'He kept accusing me of having loose morals and he hurt me by his constant criticism of what he called my dizzy mind, so I decided to get my revenge. The laugh is that I was faithful to him right up till the divorce.'

'Then why try to get me into bed?'

'Oh, well, I thought if I did that, there would be a certain something between us and John would notice . . .'

Her voice trailed away.

'I'm not going to discuss this any further,' said Hamish. 'I am here to do a job and I didn't do it very well by letting you wander off on your own. I'll go into the village tomorrow and report it to the local policeman. I couldn't phone tonight. The man would be drunk as usual. Have you any idea if it was a man or a woman who pushed you?'

Jane shook her head.

'The pillbox is quite near the hotel. Haven't you seen anyone coming and going – using it?'

'Oh, yes,' said Jane, 'some little man.'

'Description?'

Jane shrugged. 'They all look the same to me, small and bitter and prematurely old.'

'So you *do* know there's a lot of hostility against you on this island? Why on earth do you stay amidst such hatred?'

'Hamish, I barely see them, and they're cheerful enough when the health farm opens up to visitors because it means cleaning and serving jobs for the local women. They never did like me. There's been a sort of intense hatred started up just recently.'

'The Bannerman woman?'

'I can't see how she can have anything to do with it. She's always been one of the women who've actually talked to me when I've gone into the village. Look, Hamish, I've made a success of this place. People who wouldn't dream of going to a health farm in the home counties come up here. It has a romantic interest and I attract walkers and outdoor types as well as those who want to lose weight. I showed that ex-husband of mine I could do it and made him eat his words.'

'I'll let you know how I get on with my investigations tomorrow,' said Hamish. 'Good night.'

She threw him a look, half-mocking and half-appealing. One hand toyed with the long zip at the top of her housecoat and Hamish was frightened she meant to pull it down and fairly scampered from the room.

The next day, he made his way towards the village. He had hoped Harriet might have wanted to accompany him, but that lady had gone out walking with Heather, of all people.

Once again, he came across Geordie and his truck stuck on the road. Geordie, Hamish had decided, staged these breakdowns for some mad reason of his own, and so he ignored Geordie's moanings and wailings and offered to drive him. He had been unable to borrow Jane's jeep because it was insured to cover only her driving.

The truck started amiably enough. 'He likes you,' said Geordie, shaking his head. 'An odd beast.'

'Forget about the truck,' said Hamish. 'Who uses that pillbox on the beach?'

'Angus Macleod. Him and his son have a fishing boat. It wass the wan that brought yourselfs over.'

'Well, last night, someone pushed Mrs Wetherby into that pillbox and bolted the door. She could have died of exposure.'

'Och, it's all right,' said Geordie. 'Angus wass in the bar last night and he wass saying he would let herself out at midnight when he had given her a rare fright.'

'I'll be seeing Angus, then,' said Hamish grimly.

'Ye won't be able to dae that. Himself took the boat out this morn.'

Hamish stopped the truck. Geordie screeched, 'He disnae like tae be stopped fur no reason at all.'

'Forget the truck. Listen. Do you hate Mrs Wetherby?'

'Naw, I hivnae the time to hate anybody what with bringing the lobsters over frae the west and collecting the goods for people to deliver when the ferry comes in.'

'Well, she's hated nonetheless. When did it start?'

'Och, nobody likes incomers, and the wimmen are fair scandalized with the leg show she puts on, but it must hae been recently they all started cursing and blinding. Don't know what started it.'

'Well, I'll find out.' Hamish turned the key in the ignition. Nothing happened, not even a choke. 'I telt you he didnae liked to be stopped fur no reason,' said Geordie patiently.

'I'm fed up wi' your nonsense.' Hamish opened the door. 'I'm walking.'

He slammed the door behind him and strode off down the road. 'Come back!' screeched Geordie's voice. 'He's following you!'

Hamish turned around, and with a feeling of superstitious dread, he saw the truck rolling silently towards him. He stopped and the truck stopped beside him. He climbed in, checked the brakes, turned the key in the ignition, and the engine roared to life.

He drove silently into Skulag, vowing that once he had a bit of time, he would find a mechanic to check Geordie's truck.

The police station was locked. Hamish leaned on the bell for a considerable time until at last the blear-eyed constable, still in his pyjamas, answered the door.

'And they call *me* lazy!' marvelled Hamish.

'What d'ye want?' growled Sandy.

'I want you to put on your uniform and go and charge Angus Macleod with assault.'

'He's awa'.'

'Well, when he comes back.'

Sandy looked at him with contempt. 'You mean, for pushing thon Wetherby woman into the pill-box? That's naethin's but mischief. Look, Macbeth, I'm no' going tae arrest anyone. When I first got here, I arrested two o' the fishermen for stealing the council's wire waste-baskets off the jetty to use as lobster pots. The islanders gathered around the polis station calling for ma' blood and I had to climb out on the roof and sit there most o' the night. If you think I'm arresting Angus for a little bit o' fun, think again.' He slammed the police station door in Hamish's face.

Hamish strolled thoughtfully along the jetty. He could phone Strathbane and report Sandy, but he did not want to do that. There would be a full-scale inquiry and he, Hamish, would be made to look ridiculous. Besides, all the islanders, he was sure, would gang up and swear Angus had been with them all day. He saw one of the fishermen, and remembering Geordie's truck, asked him if there was a mechanic on the island.

The man stood for a long time and then decided to reply. 'There's Bert Macleod down the village. He does the MOTs and things like that,' meaning the annual Ministry of Transport checks on all vehicles over three years old.

'And where does he live?'

'Opposite Mrs Bannerman.'

Hamish walked along the village street, all too aware of the twitching curtains. Mrs Bannerman was working in her patch of front garden. She saw him and scurried inside.

Opposite her house on the other side of the street was a cottage with a shed at the side, with the legend 'A. J. Macleod, Motor Mechanic,' above the door.

He went inside. There was a pair of legs in greasy overalls sticking out from under a car.

'A word with ye,' called Hamish.

The man wriggled out and scrambled to his feet. 'Are you any relation to Angus Macleod?' asked Hamish.

'His brither,' said Bert sullenly.

'He's in bad trouble. He's assaulted Mrs Wetherby.'

'It wis jist a joke and Sandy won't be touching him.'

'No, but I'm a policeman, and if Sandy doesn't do anything about it, I can report him to head-quarters and he'll be taken off the island and you'll get a replacement who won't put up wi' your nonsense.'

Bert, a small man with weak eyes behind thick-lensed glasses, blinked up at Hamish. He jingled some change in his overall pocket and looked sly.

'We could aye come to an arrangement,' he said in a wheedling voice.

'Aye, maybe we could. Do you ken Geordie Mason, him wi' the haunted truck?'

'O' course.'

'Did the MOT, did you?'

'Last year. Naethin' up wi' it.'

Hamish looked at him cynically. He knew there were garages that would pass any old vehicle as being sound, provided the price was right.

'If you want me to leave Angus and Sandy alone, you'll do this. Tell Geordie I've said there is something wrong wi' his truck and get it in here and take it apart and make sure it's sound.'

Bert pushed back a filthy cap and scratched his head. 'It won't mind that,' he said. 'Geordie says it likes a bit of attention.'

'You're all crazy,' said Hamish in disgust. 'Just see to that truck.'

On the road back, he turned his mind to the problem of who could possibly have started the hatred for Jane Wetherby. Mrs Bannerman? Someone from the health farm? Did anyone from the health farm talk to the islanders? They had all been there two weeks before his own arrival, time enough to do damage. He would need to ask Harriet. The thought of Harriet Shaw cheered him immensely. The wind had dropped as he neared The Happy Wanderer, and snow began to fall in large feathery flakes. He stopped, amazed. He could not ever remember having seen a white Christmas. Usually it snowed a bit before Christmas and a lot after Christmas. Perhaps this too would fade away before the twenty-fifth.

A Christmas atmosphere seemed to have fallen on Jane's guests at last. They were all helping her trim a large synthetic tree in the lounge and hang decorations. Even John Wetherby was laughing as he stood on top of a ladder and tried to reach up to put the fairy on top of the tree.

When the tree was finished, Hamish took Jane aside and told her the result of his investigations. Jane clapped her hands in delight. To Hamish's horror, she called out, 'Listen, everybody! Isn't Hamish clever? He went into Skulag and found out that it was Angus Macleod, a fisherman, who pushed me into that pillbox.'

John Wetherby slowly turned round. He had been bent over a box to start bringing out the tinsel and paper decorations with which to decorate the rest of the lounge and dining-room. At Jane's words he straightened up abruptly and swivelled to face Hamish.

'You reported this to the police, of course,' he said sharply.

'Of course,' said Hamish, dreading what was going to come next.

'Then why hasn't the policeman been out here to take Jane's statement?'

'Because Angus told everyone he only did it to give Jane a fright and that he was going to let her out at midnight. Sandy refused to charge him.'

'Well, he'll bloody well have to charge him. All Jane has to do is make a complaint of assault and see he does his duty.'

'It's not so easy,' said Hamish. 'All the islanders will gang up and say that Angus was in their sight all day.'

'Forensic tests,' barked John.

'They wouldn't get anywhere,' said Hamish wearily, 'that is, if Strathbane even bothered to send anyone out here. Footprints? The tide's been up as far as the entrance to the pillbox, not to mention the howling wind sweeping any marks clear. Fingerprints? Of course Angus's would be on the bolt, for it's where he stores his stuff.'

John Wetherby stared at him long and hard and then a smile curled his lips. 'I've got it,' he said softly. 'You're a copper yourself. Not a private detective, not even a police detective. Who else, I ask you, would wear boots like that?'

Hamish looked miserably at his feet. He was wearing an old tweed sports jacket, checked shirt, and plain tie and cords. But on his feet were his regulation boots. They had been broken in long ago and were very comfortable, and the thrifty Hamish had seen no reason to waste money on shoes when the state could supply him with foot-wear.

Harriet Shaw's eyes travelled quickly from face to face. There was a stillness in the room. Heather was frankly goggling, Diarmuid was looking enigmatic as usual, the Carpenters were leaning against each other, plump shoulder against plump shoulder, but someone had let out a startled exclamation, quickly stifled. Which one had it been?

'All right,' said Hamish. 'But I *am* on holiday.'

'It was that bathroom heater,' said John, rounding on Jane. 'You silly cow. How like you to get so paranoid over a mere accident.'

'At least he found out who shut me in the pillbox,' said Jane quietly. 'Now can we all just go ahead and try to have a decent Christmas?'

Whether it was Jane's remark, whether it was the presence of a policeman among them, or whether it was because Christmas was approaching was hard to tell, but at least the next few days passed almost in tranquillity. Hamish was surprised that Heather went to great lengths to keep out of his way. He had expected to have lectures from her on the fascist police.

Harriet, too, appeared to be avoiding him. When Hamish taxed her with it, she smiled and said she was too busy catching up on some writing in her room. He took refuge in reading articles in the women's magazines collected by Jane. They ranged from the supremely sensible to the downright ludicrous, depending on the publication. In one of the trashier efforts, he found an article entitled 'Shock Tactics.' It was all about how to get the man of your choice. 'Faint heart never won fair gentleman,' he read. 'Stun him. Invite him round and put on that naughty nightie and those sheer, sheer stockings.' He put down the article, feeling slightly sad. There was something almost pathetic about Jane. It was as if she had so little self-esteem that she needed to find a personality in the pages of a magazine.

And then, on Christmas Eve, something happened that made him uneasy. He saw Jane slip a note into Diarmuid's hand. He wondered uneasily if Jane was after Diarmuid, and his heart sank. Jane was determined to seduce someone to get at John Wetherby. Did she realize that by getting at John she would have Heather to deal with? For if any affair was obvious enough for John to notice, then it would be plain as day to the horrible Heather as well.

He went to bed trying to work things out in his mind. There was a ferry arriving and leaving again on Boxing Day. He was determined to be on it. Jane needed a minder to protect her from malice, not a policeman, and she had enough money to hire one. He resolved to tell her that in the morning.

But he awoke very early, and in the distance he

heard the reassuring sounds of domestic clatter. Then he remembered that Harriet was making the Christmas dinner, which was to be served in the middle of the day. He shaved and dressed and made his way to the kitchen. Harriet was bending over one oven, taking out a tray of mince pies. A huge stuffed turkey stood ready to be placed in the other, larger oven.

'My, you've been busy,' said Hamish admiringly. She was wearing a scarlet wool dress and a frilly apron. Instead of her usual sensible walking shoes, she was wearing a pair of scarlet low-heeled pumps.

'My big day,' said Harriet, avoiding his gaze. 'Can I get you some coffee?'

'Yes, and you'd better tell me the truth about why you've been avoiding me,' said Hamish. 'Come on. If it's because I'm getting on your nerves, I'll float off like the Highland mist.'

'No, it's not that,' said Harriet slowly. She leaned her floury hands on the kitchen table. 'I became a bit worried. I am not in a position to get into any emotional entanglements, and I like to cut them off before they start to happen. That's a bit muddled, but I'm sure you know what I mean. I began to sense something there. Attraction. On my side, at least.'

Normally shrewd, Hamish should have asked her why she was avoiding any emotional entanglement, but he felt such a surge of elation that she found him attractive that common sense went out the window.

'Och, I'm not the type to get heavy,' he said.

'There is also the question of age. I am forty-five and you, I judge, are somewhere in your early thirties.'

'Is this a proposal of marriage?'

'Hamish Macbeth! Don't be silly.'

'Well, then, I suggest we continue to be attracted to each other. Friends it is,' said Hamish with a grin. 'Need any help?'

She looked at him half-ruefully. 'Yes, I could do with a bit of help. You do make me feel like a pompous fool. Friends we are. The oven's ready for the turkey, if you'd just put it in.'

'Actually, I'm thinking of leaving on the ferry tomorrow,' said Hamish after shutting the oven door. 'It hasn't been the nicest of visits. Jane needs a minder, not a copper.'

'I might leave with you,' said Harriet, 'although it will be a waste of left-over turkey.'

'Why?'

'Jane doesn't really like the idea of meat. She'll probably throw the rest away. I won't be around to make turkey hash or turkey sandwiches.'

'Then just wrap it up and I'll take it with me.'

'Hamish Macbeth, whatever for?'

'It'll go to waste otherwise. She can't offer it to anyone on the island, her being so unpopular.'

'All right, Hamish. If you are prepared to carry a turkey carcass back to Lochdubh, you are welcome.'

'How did you come to write cookery books?' asked Hamish.

Harriet worked away at the kitchen table and

told him about her writing career while pleasant smells filled the kitchen. The snow had disappeared, as it always seemed to do on Christmas Day, but there was the usual gale howling outside to intensify the air of cosiness inside.

After his pleasant morning, Hamish was prepared to find Christmas dinner a let-down – because of the nature of the guests rather than the cooking, which turned out to be superb. There was soup made from the turkey giblets, followed by the finest Scottish smoked salmon. Then came the turkey, brown and glistening, with chestnut stuffing and chipolata sausages. John carved the turkey and the atmosphere was fairly jolly. But it was Jane, not Heather, who turned things sour.

Sheila and Ian asked for second helpings and Hamish was just about to hand his plate over as well when Jane said seriously, 'All this overeating is very bad for you, Sheila. Didn't I tell you in the summer that it was not crazy diets which took off the fat but sensible exercise and eating smaller meals?'

Sheila's face crumpled. 'You're horrid,' she said.

'What do you want my wife to look like?' demanded Ian furiously. 'Some sort of girlish whore like you?'

Jane said in a maddeningly reasonable voice, 'Your affection and loyalty to your wife do you credit, Ian, but it is known as *enabling*, just like giving an alcoholic drink. I have often noticed . . .'

'Shut up, you stupid bitch,' said John. 'Don't you realize you are being downright *cruel*?'

Jane looked at him, open-mouthed.

'Here, now.' Diarmuid leaped to Jane's defence. 'It's Jane's job to see we are all healthy.'

'Not while we're her guests,' said Harriet. 'Really, Jane, you are going to turn into one of those people who pride themselves on speaking their mind while they tramp over everyone's finer feelings.'

Comforted by all the voices in her defence, Sheila took a plate of turkey from John, and then threw another metaphorical log on the already blazing fire. 'Like Heather, you mean?' she said sweetly.

'Don't try and pick on me or it'll be the worse for you,' said Heather. 'I am glad I am a woman of independent mind and haven't got a brain stuffed with rubbish from romances.'

'But you haven't got an independent mind, Heather dear.' John brandished the carving knife at her. 'It's full of Communist claptrap. You're the sort of woman who would have turned her husband and family over to the KGB, all to the glory of Joe Stalin. And furthermore, if you have such an independent mind, why do you try to dress like Jane? She can get away with wearing short frocks because she's got good legs and a first-class figure while you just look like mutton dressed as lamb.'

Harriet looked desperately at Hamish, who rose to his feet. He raised his glass. 'Merry Christmas, everyone,' said Hamish Macbeth.

Startled, they all muttered 'Merry Christmas.' Hamish remained on his feet. 'Her Majesty, the

Queen,' he proposed. All dutifully drank that one, except Heather. 'And here's to our cook, Harriet Shaw,' went on Hamish gleefully, while everyone hurriedly replenished their glasses. '*And* to our hostess.' Harriet began to giggle. 'Do sit down, Hamish. You'll have us quite drunk.'

But the sudden rush of alcohol into the systems of the angry guests worked well. The quarrels appeared to have been temporarily forgotten by the time the Christmas pudding was served.

After the meal was over, Jane led the party through to the lounge.

'Oh, dear,' murmured Harriet, for under the tree was a pile of presents. Jane had bought presents for everyone. Harriet had guessed she would, but had forgotten to warn Hamish. Diarmuid got that item of headgear usually advertised in mail-order catalogues as a 'genuine Greek fisherman's hat.' He was delighted and ran to a mirror to admire the effect. Harriet got a newfangled pastry-cutter; Sheila, a new romance called *Texas Heat*; Ian, a pair of slippers; John, a pocket calculator; Heather, a large volume entitled *The Degradation of the Working Classes in Victorian Scotland*; and there was even a present for Hamish. It was a grey-green sweater ornamented with strutting pheasants.

The guests then went to fetch their presents for Jane. 'I forgot to warn you,' whispered Harriet to Hamish. 'Have you got anything?'

Hamish suddenly remembered the bottle of perfume in his luggage. He had bought it to give to

Priscilla and had then forgotten about it, having packed it by mistake along with his shaving-kit. 'I only need a bit of Christmas wrapping,' he whispered.

Soon Jane was crowing with delight as she unwrapped her presents, although they were a singularly unimaginative set of offerings, from a cheque from her ex-husband to a record of protest songs from Heather.

'Gosh, I've eaten so much,' sighed Heather.

'A good walk is what we need.' Jane got to her feet. 'Why don't you all go ahead and I'll catch up with you?'

Heather fumbled about the coats hanging at the doorway, complaining she could not find her oilskin. 'Take mine,' said Jane. 'Save you time looking. I've got another one.' So Heather put on Jane's yellow oilskin and all of them went out into the fierce gale.

It was after they had gone a mile along the beach that Hamish realized that Diarmuid and Heather were having a monumental row. The wind snatched their words away but then the little group saw Heather smack her husband's face. Diarmuid turned on his heel and strode back in the direction of the hotel. As he passed Hamish, his face was tense and excited.

Heather strode off inland, at right angles to the beach, without a word. The others huddled together and watched her go. 'I wonder what all that was about?' said Sheila. 'I thought they never had rows – well, hardly ever.'

'Look,' said Ian, 'there's a truck coming along the beach.'

Hamish recognized Geordie's antique Fiat. It drew to a stop beside them and Geordie jumped down. He held out his hand to Hamish. 'I want tae thank you,' he said. 'I've neffer had a bit o' trouble wi' him since Macleod fixed things.'

'There you are,' said Hamish with a grin. 'It's all in the mind. Where are you off to?'

'Skulag. I've had enough o' the missus. I'm going to the bar.'

'Why don't we go with him?' Hamish asked the others. They all agreed, suddenly not wanting to go back to the health farm and spend the rest of Christmas Day with a warring Heather and Diarmuid.

'What about Jane?' asked John.

'I don't think she means to come,' pointed out Hamish. 'And besides, we never told her which way we were going on our walk.'

'Two in the front and the rest up on the back,' said Geordie.

They all rattled cheerfully on their way and were soon settled in the bar of The Highland Comfort, ignoring the hostile stares of the locals and getting quite tipsy. Geordie had said he didn't dare join them, lest the islanders damn him for consorting with 'the enemy.'

It was five o'clock when Hamish reluctantly suggested they should return. It had been so easy and companionable. The Carpenters had told stories of farming life in Yorkshire, John had related some very witty anecdotes about terrible judges, and Harriet had made them laugh with an account about being interviewed on television by an interviewer with a prepared list of questions who thought Harriet was a literary-prize winner and who had ploughed on regardless.

Geordie had disappeared, and so they all had to walk back. Hamish took Harriet's hand. He knew he was quite drunk, a rare state of affairs for him. He felt warm and happy despite the howling wind and darkness. But as soon as he saw the pink sign of The Happy Wanderer, he experienced such a sharp feeling of dread that he let Harriet's hand drop and stood still.

'What's the matter?' asked Harriet.

He shivered. 'Someone walking over my grave. Come on. Jane will be wondering what has happened to us all.'

Jane and Diarmuid were seated in the lounge in front of the fire, side by side on the sofa. They rose to meet the company. Hamish looked at both of them sharply but Diarmuid looked much as usual, and Jane seemed delighted to see them, asking if they had enjoyed their walk.

'Where's Heather?' asked Hamish sharply.

'Still out. She walked off in a huff, if you remember,' replied Diarmuid.

'She shouldnae be out in the dark on her own. She hadn't a torch.' Hamish looked worried. 'We're going to have to organize a search-party.'

'It's not late,' said Jane soothingly. 'She's probably staying away to give us a fright.'

'And she's succeeding wi' me,' said Hamish grimly. He picked up a torch. 'I'm going to look for her.'

'I'm coming too,' volunteered Harriet, not because she was worried about Heather but because she did not want to be with the others without Hamish.

'I think you ought to go too,' said John, looking at Diarmuid with dislike. 'That is, if you can tear yourself away from my wife.'

'Ex-wife,' said Diarmuid huffily. But he got to his feet and took his Barbour coat down from a hook at the door and then spent some time adjusting his new cap on his head. Not wanting to be left out of things, the Carpenters volunteered their services, and then Jane said she would go as well, for she knew the island better than any of them.

They split up outside. Harriet insisted on staying with Hamish and Sheila with her husband. Jane and Diarmuid and John looked at each other under the light of the pink sign and then, without a word, went their separate ways.

'I couldn't be on my own on an island like this,' said Harriet, keeping close to Hamish. 'It's spooky. You forget there are still parts of the world where there are no street lights, no shops, nothing but the howling wind and blackness.'

For hours they struggled through endless miles of moorland and croftland, knocking at cottage doors from time to time, asking if anyone had seen Heather, but no-one had.

It was nearly midnight when they returned, to learn from the others that Heather was still missing. Hamish went through to the phone and tried to rouse Sandy Ferguson, the policeman, but without success. He then phoned headquarters at Strathbane and ordered air-sea rescue patrols just in case Heather had been blown off some crag into the sea.

He sat up late while the others went to bed, waiting and hoping for Heather's return. In the morning, he set out at six and walked down to the village and began banging on doors and summoning all the men he could get to help in the search. Strangely, he knew there would be no difficulty. The islanders' spite did not extend to leaving some woman, possibly injured, lying out on the moors.

As dawn finally rose, he already had a line of men straggling out from the village, searching everywhere. The gale was tremendous, booming and shouting and roaring across the sky. Soon the brief daylight would begin to fade. Hamish looked up at the sky. There seemed little hope of any air rescue even getting off the landing strip in such weather.

Sandy Ferguson had sulkily joined the search. He looked more hung over than ever.

Hamish became aware that a red-haired child was studying him curiously as he searched around a large peat stack.

The boy crept closer. 'Are ye looking for her?' he whispered.

'Aye,' said Hamish. 'A Mrs Todd.'

'I saw her sunbathing,' said the boy.

Hamish looked at the white, pinched face and his eyes sharpened. 'Could you take me to where she was sunbathing?'

'Aye, I could that, but it's ower on the west.'

'What's your name, laddie?'

'Rory Sinclair.'

Hamish called to one of the men on the road, who came running up. He drew him aside. 'This boy's talking about seeing a woman sunbathing.'

'Och, Rory's daft. A wee bitty simple.'

'Still, we've got to try everything. You've got your car. Let's get the lad into it and get him to show us where he saw the woman.'

Rory climbed into the passenger seat, highly excited at the thought of a trip in a car.

'Where on the west?' asked Hamish from the back seat.

'Balnador.'

The car, an old battered Mini-Cooper, chugged its way along roads which were little more than tracks, heading to the north-west of the island. 'Vroom! Vroom!' said Rory, obviously enjoying himself hugely.

The car finally rolled to a stop. The driver said, 'This is as far as I can get to the shore.'

Hamish climbed out, helped Rory out of the front seat, and said, 'Show me where you saw her.'

The boy scampered ahead. The clouds parted

and a fitful gleam of sunlight shone on the crags of rocks ahead, sticking up like broken teeth. The boy scrambled up them like a young deer, crouching before the wind. Then he shouted something that was torn away by the gale and pointed down.

Hamish scrambled up after him and lay on his stomach on a small triangle of mossy grass. The crag overlooked the sea. Huge waves were racing in, black and green and dashing themselves on a small pebbly beach. The thunder of the waves was deafening. The whole world seemed to be in motion. Waves reared up to tremendous heights before tumbling down with a powerful roar.

Hamish put his lips to the boy's ear.

'Where?'

Again the boy pointed down.

Hamish craned over the crag. And there down below, just beyond the fanning spread of the crashing waves, he saw a woman's foot.

Balancing against the ferocity of the wind, he turned and signalled to the driver, a small figure in the distance, and waited impatiently until the man crawled up to him. 'She's here,' bawled Hamish. 'Get the doctor and get help, but take this lad away first.'

When the boy had gone, Hamish slowly began to ease his way down to the small beach.

Heather Todd lay under a curve of overhanging rock. He stooped down and felt her pulse. Nothing. He examined her head and then gently lifted it.

Her neck was broken and there was an ugly bruise on the side of it. He drew his knees up to his chin and waited, shivering, beside the dead body, for help to arrive.

CHAPTER FIVE

I hope I shall never be deterred from detecting
what I think a cheat, by the menaces of a ruffian.
—SAMUEL JOHNSON

Hamish supposed there *would* be a doctor on the
island. There must be. He stood up and stretched
and looked up at the crag above him and then at
Heather's body. The only heights on the island
were the crags at various parts of the coast. How
could she have broken her neck? The crag was only
about fifteen feet above the beach. It was no
enormous cliff with a fall on to jagged rocks.
Admittedly, if she had bounced against one of the
sharp projecting edges, that might have done the
trick.

The wind was less savage now and he could
clearly hear the sound of voices above him. Occasionally a torch beam searched him out as more
islanders began to gather. And then he heard
Sandy Ferguson's voice. 'Is that you, Hamish? I'll
send a couple of men down to collect her so that
Dr Queen can have a look at the body.'

'No, you won't,' shouted Hamish. 'Nothing has to be touched. Get him down here and bring a tent to cover the body until the pathologist arrives.'

There was the sound of swearing and then a scuffle followed by the clatter of falling debris as Sandy and a thin elderly man made their way down.

'This is Dr Queen,' said Sandy.

The doctor was a thin, spare man with a face set in lines of permanent arrogance. 'I gather you're some sort of local bobby from the west coast,' he said. 'Well, stand aside, man, and let's have a look at her.'

'Gently, now,' warned Hamish. 'Don't disturb anything.'

The doctor ignored him. 'Bring that lantern closer, Sandy,' he said. 'Mmm, yes. As I thought. She was blown off the top of the crag and broke her neck. Sad but straightforward. Get some men to take her up, Sandy, and get her put in my surgery while I prepare a report for the procurator fiscal.'

'You are not to touch her.' Hamish Macbeth stood four-square beside the body.

'Why not?'

'Because I think it might be murder. I think someone struck her a savage blow on the neck wi' a rock.'

'Dear me, don't be a fool, there's a good fellow,' said the doctor.

'I repeat: no-one touches this body until a team from Strathbane arrives,' said Hamish stubbornly.

'You have not the authority. This is *my* island,' protested Sandy.

102

'Aye, and you'll find yourself off it soon enough if I have my way,' snapped Hamish. 'I'm telling you to leave it where it is or, by God, I'll make trouble for both o' ye.'

The doctor glared at him, but snobbery came to Hamish's rescue. Had Hamish been a holidaying policeman who was bird-watching or hiking, then Dr Queen would have ignored him. But this Macbeth was a guest at The Happy Wanderer where, the doctor had learned, there was a barrister in residence. He and the other guests might back Hamish.

'Have it your way,' he said haughtily. 'But you're going to look a right idiot, wasting the taxpayers' money like this.'

Hamish turned to Sandy. 'Are you going to phone headquarters, or am I?'

'Oh, you do it, laddie,' jeered Sandy.

'Then get a tent over the body and set two men to guard it. I'll be back.'

One of the islanders ran Hamish to The Happy Wanderer. When he went into the lounge, the guests started up. There were also five of the island women there who, it turned out, worked as servants at the hotel during the season. Hatred for Jane seemed to have disappeared with the tragedy, and they were all exclaiming and commiserating in their soft island voices, changed from sinister threatening figures to a group of ordinary woman.

'This is terrible,' said Jane.

'Where is Diarmuid?'

'In his room. He's phoned his secretary, Jessie

Maclean, and told her to get up here as fast as possible. I've heard of Jessie. Seems she does everything for him, including thinking, or that's the way Heather put it once.'

'I've got calls to make,' said Hamish, and Jane led him into the office and left him.

Hamish decided to phone the bane of his life, Detective Chief Inspector Blair, and make his report to him direct. If he did not, it was ten to one that it would be Blair who would arrive anyway, and a Blair sulky that Hamish had not told him about it firsthand.

Blair gave Hamish his customary greeting in his heavy Glasgow accent. 'How are ye, pillock?'

'Listen,' said Hamish. 'I'm staying at a place called The Happy Wanderer on Eileencraig. One of the guests appears to have fallen off a crag and broken her neck, but I'm convinced it's murder.'

There was a silence, and then Blair said sharply, 'Are ye sure? Working in the holidays is a pain in the arse as it is, and ah'm no' that keen tae get the police helicopter oot on a wild-goose chase.'

'I promised if there wass ever another murder, I'd let ye in on it,' said Hamish. 'I think you ought to come and bring the works.'

'Oh, well, ah never cared much for Christmas anyways. As long as ah'm back for Hogmanay, it'll suit me. I could be daein' wi' the overtime.'

Hamish briefly gave a description of where the body was to be found, what the local doctor had said, why he, Hamish, thought it might be murder, and a brief summary of the little he knew of the Todds. Blair recorded it all and told Hamish to watch the body and that he and the forensic team should be with him in a couple of hours.

Hamish rang off and then rested his elbows on the desk and wondered if he was making a fool of himself. The wind had been savage. She could easily have been blown off that crag.

The office door opened and Harriet came in and stood looking at him quietly. 'Surely an accident,' she said.

'It could be murder, Harriet.'

'But we were all here!'

Not when we were searching for her, thought Hamish. Someone could have found her when they were out searching and struck her down.

'It's got to be investigated anyway,' said Hamish wearily. 'I've got to get back and make sure they don't move the body.'

'Give me a few minutes and I'll come with you. I can make a thermos of coffee and some sandwiches and take blankets along. No, don't protest. It's better than waiting here. There are more islanders arriving, men this time. They're all being terribly nice to Jane. It's a great pity it had to be Heather's death that brought this about. I won't be very long.'

Hamish went back to the lounge. Jane had found a long black dress and put it on. She was dispensing large whiskies to the islanders. Perhaps it was genuine sympathy, or perhaps because the news that free whisky being served acted on the Highland and Island brain wonderfully, but more islanders kept arriving every minute.

Hamish went to Diarmuid's room and quietly opened the door. Diarmuid was sitting in an armchair, staring into space.

'I'll get matters cleared up as soon as possible,' said Hamish quietly. 'Are you all right?'

'My God,' said Diarmuid in a low voice, 'I don't feel a damn thing.'

'Shock,' said Hamish. 'Do you want someone to sit with you?'

Diarmuid shuddered. 'I'd rather be alone, Hamish.'

'I'll send someone to fetch the doctor. You need a sedative to settle you for the night.'

Hamish went back to the lounge. John Wetherby came up to him. 'Can't you get rid of these people?' he asked. 'This is hardly the occasion for a party.'

'I think it's better for Jane that they stay,' said Hamish. 'It's high time they found out she's just an ordinary person like themselves.'

John made a contemptuous noise which sounded like 'garrr,' and strode off. The Carpenters were talking to some of the islanders. They did not look shocked, rather they looked happy and excited. Ian was talking about sheep, a subject close to any islander's heart, and he had a rapt audience.

Harriet came back carrying a large bag. 'Blankets and food,' she said briskly.

'Right,' said Hamish. 'Now let's see if someone can lend me a car.'

One islander, clutching a large tumbler of

whisky, cheerfully parted with his car keys and Hamish with Harriet made his way back over to the west.

The men put on guard were happy to be relieved. 'We will chust be going over to that hotel to offer our condolences,' said one eagerly.

'That's nice of them,' said Harriet when the men had left after Hamish had instructed them to find Dr Queen and send him to The Happy Wanderer to attend to Diarmuid.

'You'd be amazed if you knew how news travels up here,' said Hamish. 'They've got the wind of whisky. In another hour, an awf'y lot o' islanders will have found their way to The Happy Wanderer.'

A small tent had been erected over Heather's body, much to Harriet's relief. The wind had dropped and the tide had started to go out. They sat down on the beach a little way away from the tent, wrapped in blankets, sipping hot coffee and eating turkey sandwiches.

'If it is murder,' said Harriet suddenly, 'have you taken into account that Heather was wearing Jane's oilskin?'

'Yes, I'd thought of that. But we all knew Heather was wearing it.'

'But listen! The islanders didn't know, and Jane was wearing another of her yellow oilskins, an older one, when we went out searching. In the dark, someone with a torch bent on murder might only see the gleam of yellow.'

'Could be. But I've a feeling, if it is murder, that the intended victim was Heather.'

'Wait a bit. Diarmuid could have staged that row. Instead of going back to the hotel, he could have followed Heather. It's always the husband, isn't it?'

'Yes, quite often,' said Hamish slowly. 'But keep this to yourself. I thought Diarmuid had maybe staged that row so as to go back and be alone with Jane.'

'I don't think that can be right.' Harriet shivered and Hamish put an arm about her shoulders. 'Jane actually thought Diarmuid was a bit of a silly ass. She said he had only married Heather for her money because his real estate business was going down the tubes. She rather liked Heather's adulation for her. I can't really see Jane pinching anyone else's husband.'

'But I saw her slip him a note on Christmas Eve.'

'Oh, well, you'll have to ask him about that. Let's talk about something else. Tell me about your other cases.'

Hamish talked on and they sat huddled together while the receding sea grew quieter.

Harriet was never to forget that night, sitting on a lonely Hebridean beach with a constable's arm around her shoulders and a dead body only a few feet away.

And then after a long time had passed and both were getting sleepy, they heard the roar of helicopters. Hamish jumped to his feet and picked up the lantern and began to wave it. The forces of law and order from Strathbane had arrived.

*   *   *

Harriet watched, fascinated, for the next hour as photographs were taken and samples of pebbles and grit put into envelopes as a forensic team got to work. Detective Chief Inspector Blair and his sidekicks, Detectives Jimmy Anderson and Harry McNab, stood silent. Blair made a sour remark that Macbeth always seemed to have some female hanging about and retreated to the shelter of the helicopter which had brought him to the island and waited for the pathologist's report.

The pathologist eventually emerged from the tent. 'Well?' demanded Hamish.

'Could be,' he said laconically. 'On the other hand, ten to one she broke her neck in the fall. The forensic boys are crawling over those rocks on the way down to see if they can find anything.'

Blair's bulk appeared on the crag above their heads. 'Is it murder?' he asked.

'Maybe,' said the pathologist. 'You can get the body photographed now. The forensic team'll probably be here the rest of the night and then I'll get the body flown over to the procurator fiscal in Strathbane.'

Blair heaved a great sigh. 'Come on up, Macbeth,' he said. Blair was feeling thoroughly fed up. He wished he had not come. But Hamish had a gift for nosing out murders and Blair was frightened that, had he not come, the case might have been given to some young up-and-coming rival. Hamish and Harriet scrambled up after Harriet had neatly stowed blankets, thermos, and sandwich paper wrapping into the bag.

'Show us where this Happy Wanderer place is,' said Blair. 'We'll take the helicopter over. It's on the east, isn't it?'

Hamish nodded. He told one of the hovering islanders to take the car he had borrowed back to its owner. Harriet was tired. Everything was becoming unreal.

The helicopter lifted them over the island and landed on the beach in front of the health farm. It took a very short time, Eileencraig being only about thirty miles long and fifteen miles across at the widest part.

They all climbed down. Blair stood outraged.

All the lights in The Happy Wanderer were glaring out into the night. They could hear raucous 'hoochs' and the sound of fiddle and accordion.

'Jings,' said the pilot, sounding amused. 'They've got a ceilidh on.'

And sure enough, as Blair strode into the lounge, a full-scale party was in progress. Couples were dancing Scottish reels while the rest were clapping and shouting and cheering. Jane, face flushed, was enjoying herself, dancing a reel with a small bent man. The Carpenters were clapping in time to the music. There was no sign of either John or Diarmuid.

'Shut that bloody row!' bellowed Blair, his piggy eyes blazing with fury.

He stood blocking the doorway, a heavy-set figure of officialdom. The music stopped abruptly. As Blair, his detectives, Hamish, and Harriet

110

walked into the room, the islanders slid past them and melted away silently into the night.

'Mrs Wetherby?' demanded Blair, approaching Jane.

'Yes?'

'I am Detective Chief Inspector Blair from Strathbane. I am investigating the death of Heather Todd.' With heavy sarcasm, he added. 'I am right sorry to have broken up yer wee party.'

'You mustn't be shocked, Mr Blair,' said Jane earnestly. 'It's like a funeral, you see. People react to death in this way. It's shocking, but people are always jolly glad they're alive when anyone else has died. I read an article—'

'I'm no' interested in any article,' glowered Blair. 'Is there a room I can use for interviews? Ah'll need tae see the husband.'

'I'm afraid that is not possible,' said Jane firmly. 'Dr Queen has given him a sedative.'

'Oh aye? Well, I'll start wi' the rest o' you. Macbeth, you can go tae yer bed. I'll let ye know if ye'r' needed.'

'That's not fair,' protested Harriet. 'It's his case.'

'Neffer mind,' said Hamish, although he was furious with Blair. 'I need some sleep and so do you.'

'Efter I've interviewed her,' said Blair pompously, looking Harriet up and down.

Jane was efficiently clearing up dirty glasses and plates and stacking them on a tray. 'You can use my office,' she said, 'But you had better let me know now how it is that the constable who found the body is being barred from the investigation.'

Her upper-class accents fell unwelcomely on Blair's ears. Blair had made up his mind it was an accident and wanted to get back to the mainland as soon as possible, and he didn't want Hamish Macbeth around, throwing a spanner in the works. On the other hand, he didn't want to offend anyone who might raise a dust with headquarters. 'I was merely concerned for his welfare,' he growled. 'All right then. You can stay, Macbeth. Show us to the office, Mrs Wetherby, and we'll start with you.'

Soon he was seated behind Jane's desk, with his detectives standing respectfully behind him. That was the way he liked it. Jane sat opposite and Hamish lounged over near the door and tried not to yawn.

'Now, Mrs Wetherby . . . oh, we'd better have a copper take doon yer statement. Got yer notebook, Macbeth?'

'I'm on holiday,' said Hamish patiently.

'All right, Anderson, you do it.'

Jimmy Anderson found a hard chair in the corner and pulled out a notebook.

'I saw three policemen in the other helicopter,' said Hamish, and Jimmy Anderson flashed him a grateful look.

'I'm no' going oot tae look for them,' said Blair.

'Where is . . . the body?' asked Jane.

'At the doctor's surgery in the village,' replied Blair. 'Now, Mrs Wetherby, let us begin.'

It was then that Jane dropped her bombshell. 'The murderer meant to kill me, not Heather.'

Blair's eyes bulged. 'Whit?'

So Jane told him all about the reason for Hamish's visit and about Heather's taking her coat and Blair groaned inwardly at this extra complication. Jane then went on to describe how the others had gone out for a walk. She had meant to follow them but had got a sudden headache and had taken a couple of aspirins and gone to bed.

Hamish looked at her suspiciously. He was sure Jane had never had a headache in her life, and furthermore would have been more apt to drink herb tea if she did have a headache, rather than take aspirin.

'And then I got up,' Jane went on. The black dress had a deep V at the front. She leaned forward and stared at Blair, whose eyes goggled at the amount of rich cleavage exposed. 'Diarmuid – Mr Todd – was in the lounge and shortly afterwards I joined him. The rest, minus Heather, came back. We went out to search. I was on my own. I walked as far as the centre of the island before I gave up. I didn't see any of the other searchers until I got back.'

Blair asked her a few more questions and then dismissed her after asking her to send John Wetherby in.

The barrister appeared looking cross, dressed in pyjamas and dressing-gown. He railed on for several minutes about the 'indecent' party until he was silenced by Blair's remarking patronizingly that he had obviously never attended a Highland funeral, just as if he, Blair, had not been equally shocked by the festivities.

Blair's questions, to Hamish's surprise, were only perfunctory. His surprise increased as the Carpenters and Harriet were also questioned in the same brief manner. Where was Blair's usual hectoring and bullying?

They were finally all allowed to go to bed, Blair saying he would be back first thing in the morning.

'It nearly is morning,' said Harriet to Hamish and then gave a cavernous yawn. 'So much for a police grilling. He never really asked anything. Maybe he's saving his big guns for Diarmuid.'

'Maybe,' said Hamish, although in his heart of hearts he felt that Blair, who had worked Christmas so as to have extra time to enjoy the New Year celebrations, was only interested in getting it written off as an accident.

Blair did not turn up until ten o'clock, and with him he brought Jessie Maclean, Diarmuid's secretary, who had arrived on a fishing boat. She was a slim, pale girl in her late twenties with straight brown hair and horn-rimmed spectacles.

Diarmuid was summoned to Jane's office. Jessie went to fetch him and tried to follow him in, but Blair told her sharply that as she had reported to him as soon as she had got off the boat and he had taken her statement, he had no more need of her.

Flanked by his detectives and this time with a uniformed policeman complete with tape recorder, Blair started his interrogation. Hamish hovered by the door, watching Diarmuid's bland and hand-some face. He discovered to his surprise that he did not like Diarmuid, but why, he did not know. Heather had been so awful that all he had felt before for Diarmuid was mild pity.

'Now,' said Blair, 'we are sorry we have to put you through this, Mr Todd, but I'll need your movements yesterday.'

Diarmuid took out a pipe, filled it and lit it carefully. 'I had a row with my wife when we were out walking, I confess that.'

'What was it about?'

'Money,' said Diarmuid. 'I told her she would need to pull her horns in a bit when we got back to Glasgow. No more lavish entertaining. She took exception to this and stormed off. I walked about a bit and then returned to the hotel. There was no sign of Jane, so I read a book. Jane emerged from her room just as the others returned.' He went on to describe the search, saying he had walked miles along the beach on the eastern side of the island in front of the hotel.

'I gather from Miss Maclean that your finances are in a bad way,' said Blair.

'Well, I must admit the slump in house sales caused by the high interest rates caught me on the hop. That's why Heather and I could take such a long holiday. I dismissed the staff and locked up for the winter. I'd already sold off two of my branches, so there was just the main office left. What a mess. Thank God Jessie's here. She'll be able to sort it all out.'

'Do you inherit anything on your wife's death?'

'Nothing but a joint overdraft,' said Diarmuid.

'Was her life insured?'

Hamish listened hard.

'It was, but we didn't keep up the payments, so there's nothing from that.' Diarmuid sighed heavily.

Blair looked at him sharply. 'You know we can check on all this at the Glasgow end?'

'You don't even need to do that,' said Diarmuid a trifle smugly. 'Jessie's brought all the revelant business papers with her.'

'Why should she do that?'

'Because I phoned her and told her to.'

Blair looked at him suspiciously as he sat there smoking and frowning deeply, like an actor sitting smoking and frowning deeply. There was always something stagy about Diarmuid, Hamish thought.

The Detective Chief Inspector was worried. He did not like Diarmuid's attitude. He did not like the way he had had the foresight to get his secretary to come up, complete with papers. But Blair wanted to wrap the case up as soon as possible.

'How did Miss Maclean get here so quickly?' he asked.

'There's a night train from Glasgow to Oban, which arrives at six in the morning. I told her to get that and I phoned the hotel and arranged for one of the fishing boats to go over and pick her up.'

'You must ha' paid a fair whack to get a fishing boat to go all that way.'

'Yes, but I needed Jessie's help,' said Diarmuid patiently.

'Who was the fisherman?' asked Hamish suddenly.

'Angus Macleod. Him that usually runs trips to the mainland for Jane,' said Diarmuid.

'But,' expostulated Hamish, 'Angus Macleod iss the fellow who shut Jane up in that pillbox.'

'What's this?' asked Blair.

With a studied patience that was beginning to get on Hamish's nerves, Diarmuid explained about the 'prank.' Hamish could almost sense Blair relaxing. There was now no doubt in Hamish's mind that Blair was going to do everything to prove Heather's death an accident, and unless Diarmuid was incredibly naïve, he was helping the inspector do just that.

Blair brought the interview to an end. He said he would go back to the hotel and see if the forensic team had reported in with anything.

Hamish went in search of Jane. 'Would you mind very much if I stayed on for a bit?' he asked her. 'I am convinced that Blair is going to drop the case. I would like to stay on and see if I can discover anything.'

'Then you should,' said Jane earnestly. 'I can see you are dedicated to your job, Hamish, and you must have peace of mind or you will begin to suffer from *stress*.'

Much as Hamish had expected, Blair came back

in two hours' time and called them all together. 'The forensic team found nothing on thae rocks or on the beach.'

'Which proves,' said Hamish quickly, 'that some-one must have struck her a blow on the neck. If she had hit a rock on her road down, then—'

'Aw, shut up,' said Blair, his Glaswegian accent becoming thicker in his irritation. 'Better heads than yours, laddie, hiv discovered it was an acci-dent. Mr Todd, your wife's body has been taken to the procurator fiscal at Strathbane and can be recovered there. As I said, it was an accident, and that's that.'

Hamish followed him out. 'I don't think you really believe what you've just said,' he remarked.

'Don't you tell me what I'm thinking or no' thinking,' sneered Blair, 'and remember you're addressing a senior officer. Accident, Macbeth. That's all. Anyway, you got a tasty piece there tae keep ye warm.'

'Don't dare speak to me of Harriet Shaw in those terms,' shouted Hamish.

'Ach, dinnae be daft. I'm no' speakin' about the auld bird what writes cookery books. Jane Wetherby. Yum, yum.' And with a heavy wink, Blair got into a battered rented car. Jimmy Ander-son, at the wheel, threw Hamish a sympathetic look before driving off.

Hamish went back indoors to hear Diarmuid say pathetically that he would like to stay on for a couple of days to recover before going to Strath-bane to make arrangements for the body to be taken down to Glasgow for burial. Jessie, he said, was in the office making all the necessary phone calls.

Harriet looked at Hamish sympathetically. 'Care to go out?' she asked.

Hamish looked at her, at her clear eyes, crisp hair and firm figure and felt all his anger and irritation melt away.

'What had ye in mind?' he asked.

'A late working lunch, copper. We've had nothing to eat. Get some paper and we'll go down to the hotel and try to work out who did it.'

'So you think it might be murder as well?'

'Not exactly. But I think we ought to be sure. Blair's the sort of man who makes one want to prove him wrong.'

They walked briskly towards Skulag. The day was crisp and clear, and for once, windless. The sea shone with a dull grey light on their left. Hamish was surprised not to see Geordie's truck. Geordie, it appeared, plied his way regularly between the west coast and the village of Skulag, bringing lobsters and fish over, to be loaded on to the ferry when it arrived for delivery to the mainland, or, in summer, put in a large refrigerator shed behind the jetty to await the arrival of the next ferry. In winter, it was always cold enough to store the seafood on the jetty. He also collected goods brought over by ferry or fishing boat and delivered them to various croft houses dotted over the island. He had been working over Christmas, so it was possible he had finally decided to take a rest. The islanders were mainly Presbyterian and a lot of them would think Christmas, despite its name, a pagan festival. Hogmanay – New Year's Eve – was the real celebration.

The owner of The Highland Comfort, who acted as barman and, it appeared, just about everything else, informed them sourly that the dining-room was closed in the winter but that they could have a meal in the bar. When they were seated, he handed them two greasy menus and left them to make up their minds.

'So much for Highland delicacies,' mourned Harriet. 'Chips with everything. Hamburger and chips, lasagne and chips, pie and chips, sausage and chips, and ham, egg and chips.'

'I'll have the ham, egg and chips,' said Hamish, 'and a half pint of beer.'

Harriet settled for the same. The landlord wrote their order down carefully. 'I shouldnae hae tae do this mysel',' he complained. 'But I cannae get staff. There wass wan girl left and herself walked out on me.'

He slouched off.

'Since it'll probably take him about an hour to fry an egg,' said Hamish, 'let's get started.' He opened out a folded pad of paper and took out a pen. 'Jane Wetherby first. Any views?'

'I keep thinking about that coat,' said Harriet eagerly. 'Look, while Jane was away, we watched an Agatha Christie play on television. A woman calls in Poirot to protect her against somebody who has already tried to murder her. She invites her cousin to stay a few days with her. The cousin puts on the woman's highly coloured wrap and is killed by mistake. But it turned out that the cousin was the intended victim all along. The woman had manufactured attempts on her life to hide that fact. Jane wasn't with us. But she could have watched the show on television at her friend Priscilla's hotel.'

Priscilla. Hamish looked startled. He hadn't phoned to wish anyone a happy Christmas. They would not know what he was up to, because there would only be about two lines in the newspapers describing the accidental death of a tourist on Eileencraig. Harriet was still talking.

'So you see, Hamish, we have something of the same scenario here. Jane told you of attempts on her life. And it was Jane who told Heather to take her coat. Jane could easily have lied about that headache and slipped out of the house by the back way. The question is . . . why?'

'That brings us to Diarmuid,' said Hamish. 'Heather was older, a bore and a snob. He married her for her money and that money is gone. Did he have someone else ready to be Mrs Todd Number Two? His business is so bad, he closed down for the whole of December and a bit of January. He could have run after Heather when he was out of sight of the rest of you, stalked her over to the west coast, waited until she climbed up on that crag, and then struck her on the side of the neck with a sharp rock. All he had to do then was hurl the rock in the sea. As I told you, I saw Jane slipping him a note. Jane is a very wealthy woman with a good business. She's also got looks, and Heather had none. Worth killing for, don't you think? Diarmuid is incredibly vain, and vain men are dangerous.'

'What about John Wetherby?' asked Harriet. 'You know, Hamish, for all his sour manner, I think he's still in love with Jane. What if something made him go mad with jealousy? What if he went over the edge and struck down Heather when we were searching for her, seeing only that yellow oilskin and thinking it was Jane?'

Hamish wrote busily. 'We'd better check into John Wetherby's business affairs and find out if Jane still has a will in his favour, that is, if she ever had one. What about the Carpenters? Is there something there?'

'I don't think so,' said Harriet roundly, 'and neither do you. But I suppose they'll have to be checked into as well. But how can you do it, not being officially on the case?'

'Wonder o' wonders,' said Hamish, 'here comes our food and beer.'

As they munched their way through greasy chips, salty, fatty ham and watery eggs, and drank their flat beer, Hamish kept looking down at his notes. 'I think I should find out what was in that note Jane slipped to Diarmuid,' he said. 'But then, we should concentrate more on Heather's character. See what you can get out of that secretary. Make a friend of her.'

Harriet grinned. 'Right you are, Sherlock.'

*   *   *

When they returned to the health farm, it was to find Diarmuid had retreated to his room again. The rest, including Jessie, were watching television.

Harriet asked Jessie if she would like to take a walk and get a bit of fresh air. Jessie agreed and the pair walked outside.

Harriet studied her companion as they both strolled along the beach. Jessie was attired in a chain store's contribution to 'power dressing.' She had on a pin-striped suit, the jacket having very large square shoulder pads, and a short tailored skirt. With it, she wore a high-necked white blouse and black court shoes with low heels.

After some general conversation on the tragedy, Harriet asked curiously, 'But what about you? What will you do now? I mean, I gather Diarmuid's business was pretty much finished.'

'Oh, there'll be a lot of winding-up of affairs,' said Jessie. 'I'll be kept busy. Then I might go away somewhere. Try going to another country.'

'But you've had a month off.'

'And glad of it, too,' said Jessie waspishly. 'The Todds were a couple of slave-drivers.'

'How can that be, if the business wasn't doing at all well? I mean, what was there to do?'

Jessie stopped and looked at Harriet suspiciously and then shrugged. 'It was her that was the problem. I don't believe that woman even knew how to wipe her own backside.' The crudity sounded odd, spoken as it was in Jessie's prim, Scottish-accented, carefully elocuted vowels. 'Who do you think did all the work, setting up her "little parties"? Who typed her damn letters to this and that? Me. Even if the business hadn't collapsed, I meant to leave anyway.'

'Did she entertain much?' Harriet watched Jessie closely, thinking what a moody, rather spiteful girl she appeared. 'Oh, lots. It was all supposed to help the business. Invite the "right" people in the hope they would become clients, lavish drink and concert tickets on them. And a useless lot they were, too. Occasionally she'd net a celebrity, by playing one celebrity off against the other, you know – "Mr Bloggs is coming, Mr Biggs," and Mr Biggs is reassured that there is to be another eminent celebrity, as is Mr Bloggs when he is phoned and told that Mr Biggs is coming. Old trick, but a surprising lot fell for it. I think Mr Todd will find he hasn't a friend in the world when it gets about he hasn't any money.' This was said with a peculiar relish.

'Heather told me some very colourful stories about her upbringing in the Gorbals when it was one of the worst slums in Glasgow,' said Harriet, 'so how did she have so much money?'

Jessie sniffed. 'That was one of her lies to make her a genuine member of the left. She was brought up as an only child in a large house in Hillhead, which, in case you don't know, is a posh suburb near the university. She became left-wing to get an entrée into a society which would otherwise have rejected her – you know, theatre, writing, the arts.'

'Was Diarmuid a good boss?'

'Yes, he'd have been all right on his own, but he expected me to work for his wife as well.'

'So why didn't you leave? How long were you with them?'

'Six years. Look, they paid well, I'll say that for them. I've always wanted to live in Spain and I've kept that as my goal. Now, I'm cold. Run off and tell that copper boy-friend of yours everything I've said because that's the only reason you're marching me along this cold beach.'

And Harriet Shaw had the grace to blush.

CHAPTER SIX

... the motive-hunting of motiveless malignity –
how awful it is!
—SAMUEL TAYLOR COLERIDGE

Hamish returned to the village alone and ran Angus Macleod to earth. After lecturing the unrepentant fisherman on his disgraceful behaviour, pushing Jane into the pillbox, Hamish asked him about that phone call from Diarmuid, requesting him to pick Jessie up at Oban.

'Oh, aye, he phoned in the middle o' the evening in a rare state,' said Angus. 'Asked me to take the boat out and go tae Oban. I telt him tae get lost, but he offered me a lot and the wind was dying, so ower I went.'

'Had you ever seen the girl, Jessie Maclean, before?'

'No, first time I'd seen her.'

Hamish then took himself along the main street to Mrs Bannerman's cottage. She was furious when he questioned her about her movements on the night of the murder, but eventually said she had been at a neighbour's party. Hamish checked with the neighbour, a Mrs Gillespie, who confirmed that Mrs Bannerman had been there all evening. But the murder could have been committed earlier, thought Hamish. No pathologist could ever tell the exact time of any murder. The closest he could come to it was between about four in the afternoon and nine in the evening. Hamish asked Mrs Gillespie if she had seen Mrs Bannerman earlier and got the reply that Mrs Bannerman had also been there in the late afternoon, helping Mrs Gillespie with the arrangements for the party.

By the time Hamish returned to The Happy Wanderer, he was beginning to wonder whether Heather had actually fallen to her death after all. There did not seem to be any motive. He was told Diarmuid was still in his room. When Hamish opened the door, Diarmuid was lying flat on the bed, looking at the ceiling.

'I just want to ask you one thing,' said Hamish, 'On Christmas Eve, Jane slipped you a note. What was that about?'

Diarmuid struggled up and smoothed down his ruffled hair with a careful hand, looking across at himself in the mirror. 'Oh, that? I asked her if she had any contacts in the real estate business. I'm looking for a buyer. She gave me a note telling me to try James Baxter of Baxter, Fredericks and Baxter. James Baxter is an old acquaintance of hers. She bought the health farm from him. He's expanding his business.'

'I don't suppose you kept the note,' said Hamish suspiciously.

'Of course I did,' said Diarmuid crossly. He got up and went to the dressing-table and slid open one of the drawers. 'Here it is. I meant to give it to Jessie so that she could make an appointment for me to meet Baxter when we got back to Glasgow.'

'I'll just take this for a while,' said Hamish.

'Don't you think I have enough to bear?' demanded Diarmuid with a rare show of animation. 'Good God, man my wife's *dead*! It's an *accident*. Jessie says, and quite rightly, that you have no authority.'

'I'll hae a word wi' the lassie,' said Hamish grimly. 'But I'll be keeping this note for now.' He turned in the doorway, 'By the way, where was your wife's coat, the one she couldn't find?'

'Hanging in the wardrobe,' said Diarmuid. 'Over there. The police examined it but could find nothing sinister about it.'

Hamish ran Jane to earth in the kitchen. 'I want to ask you about Diarmuid,' he said. Jane turned a little pink and stirred something she was cooking energetically. 'What?'

'This note.' Hamish held it out. 'Did you write it?'

Jane glanced at it. He sensed she was relieved and wondered why. 'Yes, it's the name of a big estate agent,' she said. 'He wants to sell what's left of his business.'

Hamish thanked her, returned the note to

Diarmuid, and went back to the lounge, where Harriet drew him aside and repeated the conversation she had had with Jessie. 'Are you sure it isn't just an act?' asked Hamish. 'I mean, she's a wee bitch in my opinion, but there's something, well – sexy – about her. Don't you think she and Diarmuid . . . ?'

'Nothing there that I can see except a lot of contempt for her employer on Jessie's side,' replied Harriet. 'How did you get on?'

Hamish told her in a low voice the result of his investigations while John Wetherby, reading a London newspaper that had come over on the Boxing Day ferry and had been delivered along with other newspapers and magazines, suddenly glared at them suspiciously over the top of it.

'I would like to think there might have been some sort of collusion between Jessie and Diarmuid,' Hamish said. 'That contemptuous manner of hers could be all an act.'

'But she wasn't even on the island,' pointed out Harriet.

'Nonetheless, there could be something between them, and if there is, they'll drop their guard pretty soon. I cannae stand that Diarmuid. His vanity is pathological.'

'Are you sure you are not letting this dislike of Diarmuid colour your attitude?' asked Harriet.

Hamish laughed. 'I'll try not to. Where's Jessie?'

'Watching television.'

Hamish went into the television room. Jessie was sitting with the Carpenters. Hamish looked thoughtfully at the Carpenters. Was he right to dismiss them so easily as possible suspects? But he leaned over Jessie and said quietly, 'A word with you, Miss Maclean, if you please.'

She followed him out. 'We'll use Jane's office,' said Hamish.

'I asked Jane about you,' said Jessie when they were seated on either side of the desk. 'You're nothing but a bobby from some hick Highland village, and you have no right to bother my employer or me with questions. It was an accident.'

'Then if it was only an accident, you should not object to my questions,' said Hamish mildly. 'I thought Diarmuid was your ex-boss anyway.'

'I'm working for him until the funeral arrangements are over and I've promised him I'll pack up Heather's effects.'

'And then what?' asked Hamish.

She shrugged her thin shoulders. 'Probably go abroad for a bit.'

'Where?'

'Spain, somewhere like that.'

'Did Diarmuid ever have extra-marital affairs?' Her reply startled him. 'Lots.'

'And did Heather know about any of them?'

Again that shrug. 'I suppose she did. He's not good at keeping anything quiet.'

'Neither was she,' said Hamish drily. 'She must have given him a rare blasting.'

'Not she. She didn't mind what he did as long as he toed the line and paid out for all the entertainment for her parties and bridge clubs and golf clubs and what not. She wasn't interested in sex. He tried to tell her the money was running out due to the housing slump. I tried as well. But she wouldn't listen. She couldn't imagine a life where she wouldn't be lording it at one of her get-togethers and fancying herself as a leader of Glasgow society. This year was the worst.'

'Why?'

'Well, Glasgow got the award of Cultural Capital of Europe, and that meant more celebrities to try to get into her home.'

'Have you ever had an affair with him?'

'Don't be daft,' said Jessie. 'The man's useless. All he's ever really fancied in the whole of his life is his own reflection.'

Hamish told her that would be all for the moment, and once on his own, thought about her. He thought she was as hard as nails. Had she been Diarmuid's Lady Macbeth?

After dinner, he tried to question John Wetherby, but John told him acidly that he had no right to question anyone.

Hamish retreated once more to the office and phoned Detective Jimmy Anderson in Strathbane. 'You're lucky,' said Jimmy. 'Blair's off on holiday. Never tell me it's murder or he'll be having your guts for garters.'

'I'm trying to find out,' said Hamish. 'That John Wetherby. I was wondering if he's such a successful barrister after all.'

'Believe me,' said Jimmy with a laugh, 'Blair checked into everyone when he returned, just to make sure. I'll get out the file if you want to hear it.'

Hamish readily agreed.

After a few moments, Jimmy came back on the line. 'Here we are. Wetherby, John. Yes, rolling in money. Got family money as well as earned money. Very successful.

'Carpenters. There's a surprise. Now they're *rich*. Own a good part of north Yorkshire. Told friends they were looking forward to a free holiday. Like all rich people, they seem to love getting something free.

'Jane Wetherby. Good family. Not all that much money. Made a success out o' that health farm o' hers. Got a reputation of being a loose woman.' Hamish grinned: nothing like the Scottish police for using old-fashioned terms. If Jimmy had called her a harlot, it wouldn't have been surprising either. 'Not much known about her. Seems to have hundreds of dear acquaintances and not a single friend. Got a younger sister, Cheryl, who says Jane's bats.

'Harriet Shaw. Successful writer. Talks on cookery on television and radio. Moderately well off. Knew Jane slightly, I gather. Widowed.

'Diarmuid. Well, we really dug into him. Business on the skids but nothing to gain from his wife's death. Few affairs on the side but no grand passion.'

'What about the secretary, Jessie?' asked Hamish.

'She turned up on the island *after* the death. But she's been employed by him for six years. One of

132

the office staff said she ran the business, not Diarmuid.'

'So why did it become so unsuccessful? Jessie?'

'Naw. There's estate agents closing down all over the place.'

'Well, thanks, Jimmy; I'm only surprised Blair went to so much trouble.'

'Blair! It was me he got to go to the trouble, Hamish. He's that frightened you'll spring a murder on him and make him look a fool.'

Hamish thanked him and rang off. He sat chewing the end of a pencil, thinking over the case. Why? Why had anyone wanted to murder Heather? She had been a nasty woman. But there was no motive. Diarmuid did not stand to get any money from her death. Why?

He decided to stay awake that night, to wait and watch and see if anyone else also stayed awake. If, say, Jessie and Diarmuid were involved, then they would be desperate to speak to each other.

He waited until they had all gone to bed and then went into the lounge and sat down in the darkness. The hours passed slowly. There was still no wind outside and the silence was eerie.

And then, at two in the morning, just as he thought he could not keep his eyes open any longer, the light in the corridor leading to the bedrooms went on.

Hamish rose silently and crossed to the window and hid behind the curtains. He peered through the thick folds.

Jane came in, followed by Diarmuid. 'What is it, darling?' asked Diarmuid. 'What's happened?'

'I'm worried,' said Jane in a low voice. 'That secretary of yours is very much in your confidence. You must not ever tell anyone what we did.'

'Are you mad?' demanded Diarmuid. 'Get rid of that tame copper of yours, for God's sake.'

'There's a ferry the day after tomorrow,' said Jane. 'Believe me, you'll all be on it.'

'But the ferry left on Boxing Day. There won't be another for a week. I was going to hire Angus to take me across.'

'This is an Oban company. It's a small ferry which doesn't take cars, only passengers. I suggest you and Jessie get on it. You can hire a car in Oban and get from there to Strathbane.'

Diarmuid shivered. 'I'll send Jessie. I couldn't bear to see Heather's face again.'

'That's understandable. Now get off to bed, Diarmuid, and let me get to mine. I'm tired.'

He stretched out his arms. 'Jane . . .'

'Oh, leave me alone,' said Jane crossly.

Hamish waited until all was quiet and went to Harriet's room and walked in. He woke her up and then switched on the bedside light and sat on the edge of her bed.

'What is it?' demanded Harriet.

'I hid in the lounge and heard Diarmuid and Jane talking.' Hamish told her what they had said. 'So it's plain to me they arranged this murder between them.'

'No, Hamish,' said Harriet. 'Look, Jane would

134

never be involved in any murder. I've changed my mind about her. She couldn't hurt a fly.'

'Oh, no? What do any of us really know about Jane? Everyone here only knows her slightly. Diarmuid's had affairs before because Jessie told me. But just think. Jane is now rich. She's attractive. Without Heather around, he can marry her.'

'But you have no proof,' wailed Harriet. 'An overheard conversation is no proof. What are you going to do?'

'Shock tactics,' said Hamish. 'Just wait and see.'

Hamish waited until they were all gathered in the lounge after breakfast and then stood in front of the fire facing them.

'I think I have discovered why the murder of Heather Todd was committed,' he said.

There was a long silence and then a babble of outraged voices. 'It was an accident,' snapped Jane. 'You insensitive, posturing clod,' commented John Wetherby. 'Really!' screamed the Carpenters.

Hamish held up his hands for silence. 'Hear me out,' he said.

'The murder was committed by Jane Wetherby and Diarmuid Todd.' They gazed at him open-mouthed.

'It was all planned,' said Hamish. 'All they needed was the opportunity. The stage had been set by having so-called attempts on Jane's life. I was invited over to make everything more realistic. With everyone going for a walk on a wild day, Jane suggested that Heather take *her* coat so that she could claim, as she later did, that she, Jane, had been the intended victim, not Heather. Either Diarmuid followed Heather and murdered her, or he returned to the hotel and collected Jane and they murdered her together.'

Jane burst into tears and Diarmuid slowly rose to his feet, ashen-faced.

The others sat around stricken.

'I am afraid I hid in the lounge last night and listened to your conversation,' said Hamish. 'I heard you, Jane, tell Diarmuid that no-one must ever know what you had done.' He looked steadily at the weeping Jane.

Then Jane straightened and marched up to Hamish, proud bosoms jutting, head thrown back. 'I know how it must look,' she said, 'but you see . . .' She swung round and shouted at Diarmuid, 'For goodness' sake, *tell* him! Do you want to be tried for murder?'

Diarmuid just stood there, looking miserable.

Hamish had an awful feeling that his beautiful love-triangle-murder theory was falling into ruins somewhere in his head. 'You tell me,' he said to Jane.

Jane said loudly, 'We couldn't have done it. Either of us. *We were in bed together*. I was lonely. I needed someone. Then Diarmuid came back. He needed someone, too. He was dejected because his business had collapsed and Heather was treating him like dirt because he couldn't finance her little salons any longer. We had just got dressed and were back in the lounge when you all came back.

Don't you see, that's what I meant when I said no-one must ever know.' She rounded on John Wetherby. 'You're sitting there smirking; well, hear this! This was the first affair I've had in years. I was never unfaithful to you. I only pretended to be to get revenge for your insults and slights and nasty remarks. And all that's happened is that I've been to bed with some useless geek. I hate men!

"So did we bash Heather while pretending to look for her? No, we did not, for I wouldn't go anywhere with Diarmuid, not ever again.'

John Wetherby came to her side and put an arm about her waist. 'I'll sue this copper for harassment, Jane.'

'Piss off, all of you,' shouted Jane, her face contorted with rage. 'There's a ferry leaves to-morrow. Be on it. All of you!'

She stormed out.

Hamish stood silent, feeling like an utter fool. How could he have ever suspected Jane? Harriet had been right. It was his dislike of Diarmuid that had coloured his judgement.

Jane's voice had held the ring of truth.

'Let's get out of here.' It was Harriet at his elbow.

Sadly Hamish trailed out after her. The tide was out and they walked side by side over the hard white sand towards the sea. The sand was covered at low tide by an inch of water and the flat island soon disappeared behind them, leaving them walking across a mirror of water. Large clouds sailed overhead and under their feet. The absence of any feeling of land or place gave Harriet a slight feeling of vertigo. They came to a stop and stood together.

'How weird this is,' said Harriet softly. 'Standing in the middle of nowhere. In the cities there are lights and people and noise. No wonder poor Geordie is mad. I would go mad myself if I lived on this island for very long.'

'I think it hass affected my wits.' The sibilancy of Hamish's accent showed how distressed he was. He hadn't even phoned Priscilla, he had been so hell-bent on finding a murderer. Let it go, his mind told him, it was an accident. Let it go.

'Let's go down to Skulag,' said Harriet.

They walked back together. A wind sprang up and began to ruffle the surface of the water beneath their feet. They had reached the road and had gone a little way along it when an islander stopped his car beside them and offered them a lift. They gratefully accepted, remorseful Hamish glad of this sign of the islanders' new tolerance for Jane; before Heather's death, no-one would have stopped to offer any guest from The Happy Wanderer a lift.

But to his fury, when they reached The Highland Comfort, the driver stretched out a dirty paw and said, 'That'll be twa pund and fifty pee.'

'Two pounds and fifty pence for what?' demanded Hamish.

'That's whit ye'd pay for a taxi,' said the driver.

Harriet turned away as the normally mild Hamish Macbeth told the driver what to do with his car and where to put it before joining her in front of the hotel.

'That was all I needed,' said Hamish angrily.

'Whisky's what we need,' said Harriet bracingly. 'I can't drink any more of that gnat's piss they call beer.'

When they were seated by the window in the bar, each nursing a large glass of whisky, Harriet looked at gloomy Hamish and said gently, 'You mustn't give up now. You were so sure it was murder.'

'Aye, but I'm right sorry about Jane. I cannae bring to mind a time before when I made such a fool of myself.'

'It's the motive that's lacking,' said Harriet.

Hamish looked at her. 'The motive usually lies in the person themselves. That is, the murderee. What are the usual motives? Passion and money, but usually money. Of course, there's drink or drugs, but I think whoever it was put an end to Heather had all their wits about them. I cannae think what else I can do. I am sure that the clue to the whole business lies somewhere in Glasgow. Talk to me about Heather.'

'There's nothing more than I've already told you.' Harriet looked out at the jetty. Geordie's truck was parked there, and as she watched, the small figure of Geordie came round the side of it and gave the truck a savage kick in the tyre. 'Geordie's just kicked his truck,' said Harriet. 'He shouldn't have done that.'

'You're getting as bad as him.' Hamish cast an

indifferent glance out of the window. 'Go on about Heather.'

'Let me see. Oh, I know.' Harriet's face lit up. 'You'll never believe this, but I came across her reading that romance of Sheila's. She was so absorbed in it, she didn't even notice me.'

'So much for her hating romances,' commented Hamish.

'She seemed to have an obsession about them,' said Harriet. 'She cornered me and asked me to go for a walk with her, and then, as soon as we were walking along the beach, she started to grill me about how much romance writers made. I said there were romance writers and romance writers, you know, from the trash to the really top-level stuff. First-time authors in Britain often get as little as two hundred pounds a book. She said – let me think – she said that surely America was the market. What about New York publishers? I said I thought it was possible for a first-time author to get a lot of money, provided the book was a block-buster. I got the strange impression she had written one, but when I asked her, she denied it with her usual sneers.'

'We've got nothing else to go on.' Hamish sat and thought hard. 'Look, do you have a New York agent?'

'Yes, and a very good one.'

'Would he know if there was a block-buster in the offing, say, one with a background of Glasgow? What else do we know about Heather? She claimed to have been brought up in the Gorbals, that horrible slum, or it was when she was growing up. See if there's any hint of a book. It's a bit far-fetched. But if Heather had actually pulled it off and was due a large sum of money, which her husband would inherit, then Diarmuid might find it worthwhile to push her off that crag after breaking her neck.'

'So back to Diarmuid. Are you sure . . . ?'

'No, I am not letting my dislike colour my judgement this time. Could you phone your agent?'

'All right,' said Harriet. 'So long as Jane gives me permission.'

When they arrived back at The Happy Wanderer it was to find the place wearing an air of mourning caused more by Jane's desire to get rid of her guests than by Heather's death. It was a new Jane, tight-faced and brisk. She snapped at Harriet that, yes, she could use the phone in the office provided she paid for the call.

Hamish waited anxiously in the deserted lounge. The other guests were hiding in their rooms, either to pack, but mostly, he guessed, to keep out of Jane's way.

Harriet emerged from the office, her face shining. 'Where can we talk?'

'Television room,' said Hamish. 'I don't think there's anyone in there.'

They walked in together. For once the television set was silent. 'My agent says there's a block-buster all right, but he doesn't know who it's from or what it's worth, or what it's about. But it might just have a Scottish background. He says he'll ask around. I've to phone back in a couple of hours.' Elated, Harriet gave Hamish a kiss, but he was too absorbed in this new information to take much notice of it.

The next two hours seemed to drag past. They sat and watched a rerun of a Lassie movie without either of them seeing much of it. Then Harriet rose and went to phone her agent again.

'Come with me, Hamish,' she said. 'Let's see what he has found out.'

Hamish waited, tense, while she spoke to her agent again. Finally she put down the phone and took a deep breath. 'Oh, Hamish, he found out the publisher and editor responsible for this book, but in fairness he cannot be expected to be told the details of a book not yet published. But – get this! The word is that the advance was half a million dollars!'

Hamish performed a mad, erratic sort of Highland fling round the room while Harriet called the New York publisher and got through to the editor who was handling the book. Hamish stopped his cavorting and listened. He quickly gathered that the editor was amazed that a stranger should ask such questions about an unpublished book. He grabbed the phone and introduced himself. 'I am a policeman investigating a death in Scotland,' he said. 'The name of the dead woman is Heather Todd. Is that, by any chance, the name of the author?'

'No,' said the editor reluctantly. 'I can at least

tell you that much. Heather Todd is not the name of the author.' Hamish thanked her nonetheless, and said he would be most grateful if he could call again. She agreed and he sadly put down the phone.

'Damn,' he said, 'I'm now sure there's something there. Damn. If only I could get to Glasgow.'

'We're leaving tomorrow. We could go together,' said Harriet eagerly.

'I'll need to find out if one of my relatives can put me up,' said Hamish cautiously. 'My mother's from Glasgow.'

'Be my guest,' said Harriet. 'I'll get us both hotel rooms.'

'But hotels are awf'y expensive,' protested Hamish.

'Don't worry. I'm enjoying this. Say yes, Hamish. You wouldn't want the murderer to get away with it, now would you?'

'All right.' Hamish capitulated. 'If you're sure.'

The guests assembled on the wind-swept jetty at dawn the following day. 'Going to be a rough crossing,' volunteered John Wetherby, practically the first words he had said to anyone since Jane's outburst. Jane had run them all to the jetty in relays and had left without saying goodbye to any of them.

Hamish saw Angus Macleod walking up the jetty and went to meet him. 'I've been thinking,' said Hamish, 'when you went to get Jessie Maclean, was there any other passenger?'

'No, only herself,' said Angus.

'I don't suppose you do these passenger trips often. I mean, the islanders will usually wait for the ferry.'

'Aye, that's right. The only private passenger I've had was that sulky bitch o' a maid from the hotel.'

'When was that?' asked Hamish sharply.

'Och, when I wass going to pick up that Jessie female at Oban. The maid heard I wass going and asked me to take her across.'

'What did she look like?'

'Red hair and a fat face.'

Hamish walked back to join Harriet. 'Do you remember the first time we went to the bar in Skulag?' he asked.

Harriet nodded.

'Do you remember that maid at the hotel? She was just about to come down the stairs when she saw us and darted back.'

'Yes, I remember.'

'Get a good look at her?'

'Good enough. She was fat with red hair. Why?'

'I thought I was on to something for a moment. When Angus went over to pick up Jessie, he took that maid across to Oban. I was hoping for a moment it might have been Jessie herself, trying to fool us.'

'But it couldn't have been Jessie, even a Jessie in disguise,' said Harriet.

'Why?'

'Because immediately after Heather was found

144

dead, Diarmuid phoned Jessie in *Glasgow*.'

'Aye, I'm grasping at straws. Here comes the ferry.' Hamish pointed out to sea, where a small boat was bucketing through the waves.

'And here comes Jane,' cried Harriet.

The jeep drove on to the jetty and Jane climbed out. She was wearing a pair of jeans which looked as if they had been painted on, high-heeled sandals, and a low-necked blouse worn under a short blue jacket.

She approached the shivering group with hands outstretched. 'My dear friends,' she cried. 'I could not possibly let you go like this. I have been in communion with my inner being and found peace. I do not bear any resentments, even to you, Hamish Macbeth. Let us all shake hands and part friends.'

Only John Wetherby made a sound of disgust. Sheila hugged Jane to her maternal bosom and thanked her for her hospitality with tears in her eyes. Diarmuid shook hands with Jane but did not raise his eyes to her face. Jessie gave her a firm handshake and the rest followed suit.

'I'll stay if you like,' said John Wetherby harshly.

'I'll be all right,' said Jane, the smile of rather fixed serenity she was wearing fading, to be replaced by a puzzled look. 'Why?'

'I've got two more weeks' leave and I can't stand the idea of you being here on your own.'

'All right then,' said Jane, a genuine smile illuminating her face.

'Oh, dear,' said Hamish, watching the odd couple

145

walk off together to the jeep. 'I hope I'm not barking up the wrong tree.'

The ferry bumped against the jetty and bucketed up and down as they walked on board, carrying their luggage. Hamish and Harriet stood side by side at the rail, watching fish and lobsters being loaded on. 'Where's Geordie with his load, I wonder?' said Hamish.

'Here he comes.' Harriet pointed. The Fiat truck was racing down the village street. It hurtled on to the jetty. They could see Geordie's face behind the wheel contorted with fear.

The truck kept on going, plunged over the corner of the jetty, missing the end of the ferry, and sank into the sea like a stone.

Hamish ran down the gangplank, tearing off his coat as he went. He was about to plunge into the sea when Geordie's head appeared above the waters, bobbing like a cork. He swam to the iron ladder at the side and crawled up it, dragged the final few rungs by helping hands.

'What happened?' demanded Hamish.

'He tried tae kill me,' said Geordie. 'But I got the better o' him. Himself's dead now.'

'Was your truck insured?' asked Hamish.

'Tae the hilt, man,' panted Geordie. 'Tae the hilt. I'll hae a bran'-new beastie soon enough.'

Hamish darted back to the ferry and ran on board, picking up his coat on the way.

The gangplank was pulled up, the ropes released, and the ferry chugged out to sea.

'He shouldn't have kicked it,' mourned Harriet.

'Havers,' said Hamish bitterly. 'That brother o' Angus's tricked me and did a shoddy job.'

But Harriet said nothing. She leaned on the rail and watched until the small figures gesticulating around Geordie slowly disappeared from view.

CHAPTER SEVEN

Vanity, like murder, will out.
—HANNAH COWLEY

Glasgow. Hamish was bewildered.

He had not visited the city in years. Everything seemed to have changed. Landmarks he had known as a child were gone for ever. What of St Enoch Square, which was once commanded by the station hotel, the very epitome of Victorian architecture? All gone, down to the tin advertisement which used to be on the wall opposite the Renfrew bus stop: 'They Come As a Boon and a Blessing to Men, The Pickwick, the Owl, and the Waverley Pen.' Now there was a large glass pyramid, very much like the one outside the Louvre in Paris, but housing a shopping centre covering the whole area of the square.

He and Harriet had left their bags in a small hotel in the Great Western Road and had taken a taxi to drive them about the city. They dined in an Italian restaurant after their tour, Harriet saying they should have an early night and start their investigations in the morning. Diarmuid had hired a car in Oban and had gone, after all, with Jessie to Strathbane to make arrangements for Heather's body to be taken south to a funeral parlour in Glasgow.

Hamish said good night to Harriet outside her hotel room. All of a sudden he found himself remembering that impulsive kiss she had given him and wondering if he could have another. But by that time, she had closed the door. He was strongly attracted to her, that he realized, and then, hard on that thought, he remembered Priscilla. He went to his own room and dialled the Tommel Castle Hotel.

To his amazement, he was told Priscilla was not back yet. He asked for Mr Johnson and soon the hotel manager of the Lochdubh Hotel was on the line. 'How're you getting on?' asked Hamish.

'Just fine,' said Mr Johnson. 'Everything's running like clockwork.'

'Not having any troubles with the colonel?'

'Och, no, I just get on with the work, Hamish, and ignore his tantrums. I'm thinking of working here permanently.'

'And what has Priscilla to say to that?'

'Actually, it was her idea. She phoned up at Christmas, worried about what was happening, and when I told her everything, despite her father's frequent interference, was running all right, she suggested I stay on. Suits me. The pay's a damn sight better than at the Lochdubh. When are you coming back?'

'Shortly,' said Hamish. 'I'd better phone Priscilla. Still at Rogart?'

'Aye, still there and having a grand time, by the sound of it.'

Hamish then rang his mother and apologized for not having called sooner, and after asking about various members of the family, asked to speak to Priscilla. 'I'm afraid you can't,' came his mother's voice. 'She's gone off tae the pub with your dad and his friends for a drink.'

Hamish briefly tried to imagine the elegant Priscilla propping up some Highland bar with his father and friends and found he could not.

'Where are you, son?' asked his mother.

'In Glasgow.'

'At Jean's?'

Jean was Hamish's cousin. 'No,' said Hamish, 'I'm at the Fleur De Lys Hotel in the Great Western Road.'

'What are ye doing there? It's awf'y expensive.'

'Och, it's chust a wee place,' said Hamish, taking in the luxury of his bedroom surroundings for the first time and feeling like a kept man.

'No, no, I read an article aboot it,' came his mother's voice. 'How can you afford a place like that?'

Hamish found himself blushing. 'It's a long story, Ma. I'll tell ye all about it when I get home.'

He talked some more and then rang off. He undressed, got into bed and lay awake for a long time, thinking about the case; and the more he thought about it, the more he decided it must have been an accident and that the weird atmosphere of Eileencraig had put ideas of murder into his head.

But in the morning over breakfast, he found Harriet was anxious to start the investigations. 'I think we should call on Diarmuid,' she said. 'Where does he live?'

'Morris Place, as I recall.'

She took out a street map and studied it. 'Why, that's just around the corner. We can walk there.'

Morris Place turned out to be a small square of Victorian houses, mostly divided into flats, but Diarmuid, it transpired, owned a whole house. They rang the bell and waited.

After some time, Diarmuid opened the door. He was impeccably dressed in a pin-striped suit, white shirt, and striped silk tie.

'Going out?' asked Hamish.

'I was thinking about going down to the office,' said Diarmuid, blocking the doorway, 'although I'm pretty tired. I got back from the north in the small hours of the morning. What are you doing here?'

'We just wanted to ask you about Heather.'

He heaved an impatient sigh and reluctantly stood back, allowing them to enter. He then led the way to a sitting-room on the first floor. It was thickly carpeted and had a green silk-covered three-piece suite, both armchairs and sofa being ornamented with silk tassels. Heavy green silk fringed curtains were drawn back to let in the pale, grey daylight. A gas fire of simulated logs was flaring away on the hearth. In one corner of the room there was a bar. A low coffee-table stood in front of the fire, its polished oak surface protected with coasters depicting paintings by Impressionist artists. Diarmuid ushered them into chairs and then sat down, adjusting his handsome features into what he obviously considered an expression of suitable grief.

Hamish's first question appeared to surprise him. Was Heather writing a book? Diarmuid said no, although he added that she was always scribbling away at things. 'If she had written a book,' said Diarmuid, 'then she would have got Jessie to type it. Jessie typed all her letters.'

Hamish looked at him curiously. 'Jessie was *your* secretary. Didn't she resent having to work for your wife as well?'

'Oh, no, she's a good girl, and besides, Heather paid her separately.'

'Where is she now?'

'At home.'

Hamish took out a small notebook in which he had written all the phone numbers and addresses of his suspects. 'Would you mind if I used your phone and gave Jessie a call?'

'Help yourself,' said Diarmuid, jerking his head to a white-and-gilt model of an early telephone which stood on a side-table by the window.

Hamish rang Jessie. When she answered, he asked her if Heather had ever asked her to type any pages of manuscript.

'No,' said Jessie harshly. 'Anything else? I'm busy with the funeral arrangements.'

Hamish said no, nothing for the moment, and thoughtfully replaced the receiver.

There seemed to be nothing else to ask Diarmuid. Diarmuid appeared to have forgotten all about going to the office as he ushered them out.

'I feel like giving up,' said Harriet gloomily as they left Morris Place. 'It's such a long shot, Hamish.'

'I'd like to try that editor in New York again,' said Hamish. 'I've got an idea.'

'Well, we can't phone until at least three in the afternoon, when it'll be ten in the morning in New York,' pointed out Harriet. 'I've got some shopping to do. I'll meet you back at the hotel this afternoon.'

Hamish wandered about the city and then ate a solitary lunch, although his mind was not on what he was eating. Bits and pieces of scenes floated through his mind. Jane flushed and angry. John Wetherby electing to stay with Jane. The Carpenters, fat and miserable, trailing off to the station in Oban. Jessie, cool and competent, going off to hire a car in Oban. Diarmuid, relying on his secretary to do everything.

When Harriet came to his hotel room at three in the afternoon, Hamish began to speak immediately, as if he had been discussing the case with her all through lunch. 'Look, what about this? Heather actually succeeds in writing a block-buster.

Jessie types it and sends it off . . . but she puts her *own* name on it.'

Harriet looked doubtful. 'Would such as Jessie recognize a block-buster? Then we're back to means and opportunity. Jessie was not on the island when Heather was killed.'

'But Diarmuid was,' said Hamish. 'That brief fling with Jane could have been a blind.'

'He'd need to have been awfully fast to follow Heather all the way over to the other side of the island, run all the way back, and then hop into bed with Jane,' pointed out Harriet. 'Then striking her down in the dark when he was supposed to be searching for her – well, that's hardly premeditated, and if there's money for a book involved, her death would have to be worked out carefully before-hand.'

'There's something there,' muttered Hamish. 'I can *feel* it.'

He picked up the phone and dialled the editor in New York. 'I'm sorry to keep bothering you, but it's terribly important that I find out who wrote that book I was asking you about.'

'Look, all right, all right,' said the editor, 'I'll give you the author's name. It's Fiona Stuart.'

'Her address?'

The editor's voice was terse. 'Sorry, can't do that.'

Hamish sadly replaced the receiver. 'It's no go. The book was written by someone called Fiona Stuart. Of course it could be a pseudonym.'

'Give up, Hamish,' said Harriet. 'I'm beginning to think it *was* an accident.'

'Just one more try,' begged Hamish. 'Let me speak to that agent of yours.'

Harriet sighed but phoned her agent in New York and told the surprised man that a Highland constable called Hamish Macbeth wished to speak to him about that block-buster.

'Well, you're in luck,' said the agent as soon as Hamish was on the phone. 'The advance publicity is out. It's a saga of vice and crime and passion in the Highlands of Scotland, purple prose, I gather, at its worst. It's a story about a sensitive heroine who is raped by some Highland lord in Chapter One, gang-raped by yuppies in Chapter Two, mugged in Chapter Three. Falls in love with the villain in Chapter Four, and eventually, after bags of sex and mayhem, meets her true love in time for a steamy clinch in the last chapter, her true love being the one who raped her in Chapter One. It's called *Rising Passion* and is reputed to out-Jackie Collins. Fiona Stuart is the name of the author.'

Hamish put down the phone and told Harriet what her agent had said. 'Hardly a romance,' he commented.

'That's romance these days,' said Harriet drily. 'I bet it all bears no relation to the Highlands whatsoever, and what woman in her right mind would fall in love with a man who'd raped her?'

Hamish put his head in his hands. 'There must be some connection.' He phoned the editor again. 'I told you and told you,' snapped the editor, 'I can't tell you anything about her. Why don't you phone her agent, for Chrissakes?'

'Can you give me the name of her agent?' asked Hamish. He waited. He was not hopeful at all. He expected the editor to read him out the name of a New York agent. Her American voice twanged over the line. 'Here it is. Jessie Maclean, 1256b Hillhead Road, Glasgow.'

'Thank you,' said Hamish faintly. He put down the phone and turned to Harriet. 'Jessie's the agent. How does that work?'

'Easy!' cried Harriet, looking excited. 'All my money goes to my agent. He takes his percentage and then sends the rest to me. If he decided to cash the money and disappear abroad, there's nothing I could do about it. Jessie takes Heather's book and acts as agent. She tells Heather she's sent it off to a New York publisher. Maybe, if she was shrewd enough, she'd send several copies round the New York publishers and then play one off against the other. Then she gets the stupendous offer of half a million. She doesn't tell Heather, but she knows the minute the book is published, Heather would know about it.'

'But Heather might never have known about it,' said Hamish. 'She – Jessie, I mean – could just sit back and not offer it to any publisher in Britain. That way there would be a good chance that Heather would never find out about it being published in America.'

'But don't you see, Hamish, for half a million she probably sold the world rights.'

'Aye, but wait a minute, for that sort of money, wouldn't any editor want to talk to the author?'

'Doesn't need to. All the agent has to say is that the author is very retiring, so retiring she's written under a pseudonym. Jessie can cope with the copy-edited manuscript and the galleys and all that.'

'So we've done it,' said Hamish, clutching his red hair. 'But how do we prove it? There's no Fiona Stuart. It must be Heather's book and Jessie pinched it. But proof? All Jessie has to say is that she wrote the book herself under an assumed name and acted as her own agent. There's no law against that. And even if we could prove it was Heather's book, how could we tie Jessie in with the murder? She wasn't on the island. She didn't know about Heather's death until Diarmuid phoned her.'

'Wait a bit,' said Harriet. 'I've just had an idea. Listen to this. Diarmuid's the sort of weak man who has always had his life run for him by two women, Heather at home and Jessie in the office. Such a man likes to, pretend he's the one who makes all the decisions. What if Jessie *phoned him*?'

Hamish looked at her silently for a long moment and then phoned The Happy Wanderer. It was a bad line and Jane's voice sounded tinny and very far away. Hamish clutched the phone hard as he asked, 'Did Diarmuid receive any phone calls on the night Heather's death was discovered?'

157

'He received one from some woman,' came Jane's voice. 'He took it in my office.'

'So far so good,' said Harriet when Hamish told her. 'But she wasn't on the island.'

They argued on about the pros and cons of the case until Harriet suggested they should see a movie and take their minds off it and return to the problem afresh. But nothing new occurred to either of them. Again, outside her door that night, Hamish wondered whether to try to kiss her, but again she had closed the door on him before he could summon up the courage.

Hamish lay in his bed, tossing and turning, thinking about Eileencraig. He fell into an uneasy sleep about two in the morning, and in his dreams he was being forced off the jetty by Geordie's truck while the maid from The Highland Comfort stood and laughed. He awoke abruptly and switched on the bedside light. That maid, glimpsed briefly, in the shadowy darkness of the stair. Fat with red hair. Wait a bit. What of a Jessie minus horn-rimmed glasses, with pads in her cheeks to fatten them and a red wig on her head? He could hardly wait for breakfast to expound this latest theory to his Watson.

'Won't work,' said Harriet. 'The hotel would ask for her employment card.'

'Not necessarily,' said Hamish. 'Goodness, if all the employees in hotels in Britain had to have employment cards, well, there'd be self-service. And The Highland Comfort must find it nearly impossible to get staff.'

'I can't buy that,' retorted Harriet. 'There's little enough work on these islands as it is. Look at all the women eager to work for Jane.'

'That's different. I bet Jane pays high wages. It's no use phoning up the owner of The Highland Comfort because he's not going to admit to a copper that he hires staff without employment cards. The owner's also the barman and he was complaining about having to do everything himself. Come on, Harriet, we're going to search Jessie's desk.'

Diarmuid was at home. He looked surprised at being asked for his office keys but surrendered them without too much of a fuss, which Hamish thought was highly suspicious, because surely a man would expostulate over a continuing investigation by a Highland bobby when his superiors had said the case was closed.

The estate office was in St Vincent Street in the centre of Glasgow. Already it had a depressed air of failure about it. Outside, above the street, Christmas decorations winked on and off, intensifying the shadowy gloom of the deserted office.

Harriet switched on the lights and looked about. 'Well, this is easy. Her desk has her name on it. It's probably locked.'

But the desk drawers slid open easily. Typing paper and carbons in the top drawer, headed stationery in the second, files in the third containing correspondence to do with the sale of houses.

'Nothing,' said Hamish, disgusted. 'Absolutely

nothing. We'd better take the keys back to Diarmuid.'

A grey drizzle was falling. Christmas was past and people were getting ready for the New Year's Eve celebrations still to come, but the city wore a tired, tawdry air, as if the Calvinistic ghosts of Glasgow were frowning at all this leisure time. The shops were full of people changing gifts and people clutching bits of toys which they had been supposed to assemble at home, but whose instructions they could not follow, probably because the instructions had been badly translated from Hong Kong Chinese. Christmas had done its usual merry work of setting husband against wife, relative against relative, and spreading bad will among men in general. People looked overfed and hung over and desperately worried about how much they had already spent.

A drunk man on the corner was singing, 'Have Yourself a Merry Little Christmas.' It sounded like a sneer.

'I hate this time of the year,' said Hamish. 'Hardly any daylight. I wish they'd make Christmas a religious festival and stop all this nonsense of decorations, cards, and gifts. A waste of money.' Then he blushed, because he was staying in Glasgow at Harriet's expense and did not want her to think him mean.

'The trouble with Christmas,' said Harriet, 'is that everyone somehow wants to recapture the glitter and magic of childhood, and it never happens if you look for it. I sometimes think that the people who spend Christmas serving meals to the homeless get the best out of it. Easter's a different matter, but Christmas will always be a pagan festival. The Americans have the best festival – Thanksgiving. No stupid presents, just a good dinner and thanks to God, that's the way Christmas should be.'

And having thoroughly depressed each other, Hamish and Harriet made their way back to Diarmuid's to return the keys.

Diarmuid seemed almost glad to see them this time. He insisted they come indoors and join him for a drink. Harriet privately thought that the sheer relief of never having to see his wife again had hit him at last. As they sat and talked, Hamish discovered to his amazement that Diarmuid thought his investigations merely a matter of police form. 'I never knew you chaps were so thorough,' said Diarmuid, sipping a large whisky. 'And all because of an accident.'

'Well, just to be even more thorough,' said Hamish, looking about, 'could I inspect Heather's things?'

'I gave her clothes to Oxfam,' said Diarmuid. 'Is that what you mean?'

He was wearing an open-necked shirt with a silk cravat. He felt the cravat and a worried frown marred his good looks. He stood in front of the mirror over the fireplace and carefully straightened his cravat. He looked at his reflection in the glass and slowly smiled. Hamish thought that Diarmuid had forgotten their very existence. He was looking at what he loved most in the world.

'Not clothes,' said Hamish. 'I was thinking more of paper and notebooks.'

'Mmm?' Diarmuid turned as reluctantly away from his reflection as a lover does from the face of his beloved. 'Oh, Jessie was round yesterday afternoon and cleaned the place up. She's got a kind heart. I couldn't bear to do it myself.'

'And where did she put the stuff?'

'Into a couple of big garbage bags. Why?'

'Where are the garbage bags?' said Hamish, getting to his feet.

'Downstairs, ready for collection. As a matter of fact, the garbage truck should be along about now. What . . . ?'

He looked in amazement as Hamish and Harriet ran from the room. Then he turned back to the glass and practised a slow, enigmatic smile. He thought that if he could raise one eyebrow like Roger Moore, it would enhance the effect.

Hamish, with Harriet behind him, hurtled out into the street. A small man was just heaving up two bags of garbage to put into the crusher.

'I want these back,' shouted Hamish.

The man hurled them down on the pavement, shrugged and followed the now slowly moving garbage truck along the street.

'Treasure trove,' said Hamish. 'Let's get these back inside and hae a look.'

Diarmuid was still practising how to raise

that eyebrow as they entered the sitting-room, Hamish holding the two bags.

'We'll chust go through these,' said Hamish.

'Mmm.' Diarmuid did not even turn round. There must be some way he could achieve it, but try as he would, both eyebrows kept going up at the same time.

Hamish opened one bag and Harriet the other and they began to sift through the papers. Then Hamish whistled through his teeth. 'Look at this.'

Harriet took the proffered page.

There was no doubt, it was part of a steamy novel. He took it from her and asked Diarmuid, 'Is this your wife's handwriting?'

Diarmuid turned reluctantly away from the mirror. 'Yes, that's Heather's, all right. What's this all about?'

'Did you really call Jessie to get her to come to Eileencraig?' asked Hamish. 'Or did she phone you?'

Diarmuid looked uneasy. 'Well, it's hard to remember. I was in shock.'

'It's verra important!'

'Well,' mumbled Diarmuid, 'she did phone me, as a matter of fact, just to find out how I was getting along, and I told her about Heather's death and she said she would come up right away. She asked me to phone and arrange for a boat to collect her at Oban.'

Without asking his permission, Hamish picked up the phone and dialled Jessie's number. There was no reply. 'Come on,' he said to Harriet. 'I've an awful feeling she's gone.'

They took a taxi the short distance to Jessie's. It turned out to be a basement flat. He did not even bother to ring the bell. There was a forlorn, deserted air about the place. A woman was leaning against the railings outside talking to another woman. Hamish approached them.

'Have you seen Miss Jessie Maclean this morning?' he asked.

'Aye,' said one of the women placidly.

'Do you know where she was going?' Hamish demanded. 'Shopping?'

'No' unless it was shop*liftin*',' said the woman and her friend laughed heartily at her wit. 'She hud two suitcases. Yes, she left aboot an hour ago wi' her man.'

'What man?'

'Her fella. An accountant, I think that's what she said.'

Hamish thought hard. Spain! That was where she had said she might go. He turned to the woman again. 'May I use your phone? I am a policeman.'

'He must be in trouble again, Betty,' said the woman's friend.

'In trouble? What's this about trouble?' asked Hamish feverishly.

'Her man, her boyfriend. He'd done a stretch in prison, I know that,' said the woman called Betty, 'because Mrs Queen doon the road's son used tae go tae school wi' him and recognized him and knew all aboot him.'

'Phone, please,' begged Hamish.

'I'll take him in,' said Betty to her friend. She led Hamish up to the front door above Jessie's basement, opened it with her key and let him into a dark hall. Hamish and Harriet waited in an agony of impatience while she fumbled with the key to the door of her ground-floor flat.

'In the hall on the table,' said Betty.

The hall was actually a dim corridor. Hamish searched through the phone book and then dialled Glasgow Airport. 'Yes,' came the metallic voice from the other end in reply to Hamish's question. 'There's a plane due to take off for Spain. It's a charter flight delayed for mechanical reasons, but expected to leave any minute now.'

Hamish asked to be put through to airport security and introduced himself. 'Find out if there's a Jessie Maclean on the flight to Spain, that charter flight.'

There was a long wait and then he was told there was no-one of that name on the flight. He turned to the woman who was standing in the hall with a small pocket calculator, obviously working out how much to charge him for the call. 'What's the boyfriend's name?' he demanded.

'Macdonald,' she said. 'Willie Macdonald.'

Hamish spoke quickly into the phone and then waited impatiently.

Back came the reply after five agonizing minutes. 'Yes, there is a Mr and Mrs Macdonald on board.'

'There's a murder suspect on that plane,' said Hamish. 'Get Mr and Mrs Macdonald off it and keep them at the airport.' Harriet, listening, heard the voice at the other end quack indignantly.

'Yes, yes,' said Hamish. 'I'll get the proper authority. Don't let them get away!'

He put down the phone and said to Harriet. 'Let's go.'

'Whit about paying for the call?' demanded Betty. He handed her a pound note and, dragging Harriet after him, ran out and down the street, looking for a cab. It was Hogmanay, New Year's Eve, he thought. There would be very few, if any, free cabs about. And then he saw a taxi with its light on rounding a corner and raced for it, with Harriet tumbling after him. He told the cabby to take them to police headquarters.

'How are you going to manage it, Hamish?' asked Harriet anxiously. 'You've no proof. I mean, you've proof that she pinched Heather's book but no proof she murdered her.'

'I'll get proof,' said Hamish, leaning forward and willing the cab to go faster.

At Glasgow police headquarters there were more delays while a detective sergeant phoned Strathbane to establish Hamish's credentials. But Hamish was lucky, Blair was still on holiday, and it was Jimmy Anderson, slightly drunk, who said that Hamish Macbeth was Scotland's answer to Kojak, and if he said there was a murderer at Glasgow Airport, then there surely was.

Soon Harriet found herself crammed into a police car along with Hamish, two detectives, and a policewoman while a carload of four policemen followed behind. They had only gone a little way when Hamish shouted, 'Stop!'

The detectives stolidly watched Hamish Macbeth hurtle into a hairdressing salon called Binty's Beauty Parlour. 'Whit's he daein'?' asked one laconically. 'How should I know?' retorted the other. 'Them Highlanders are all daft. Ye cannae figure oot the way their minds work. Maybe it's the mountains. Something tae do wi' the altitude. It affects their brains. Maybe he wants tae look nice for the arrest and is getting his hair cut.'

Hamish emerged carrying a paper bag and climbed back into the police car. The detective, driving, said with heavy sarcasm, 'Any mair shopping you would like to do?'

'No,' said Hamish. 'Chust make it quick.'

The detective put on the siren and off they went again. Harriet clutched Hamish's hand hard as houses streamed past under the winking lights of the Christmas decorations. At one point, they had to swerve wildly to avoid a drunk weaving across the road. Glasgow had obviously started the New Year's celebrations early.

Hamish gave the detectives an outline of his investigations and Harriet could practically feel disbelief emanating from the square shoulders of the detectives in the front seat, detectives who were used to drunken murders, savage gang fights on the housing estates, but not to sophisticated rigmaroles about books.

Fortunately, it was only a short trip to Glasgow Airport. Harriet blinked in the lights as the detectives, who obviously knew where they were going, led them along a corridor away from the staring passengers and into a room marked 'Security.'

And there was Jessie Maclean with a tall, weedy man sitting beside her. On a long table in front of them were their suitcases.

Jessie turned white at the sight of Hamish, but she said nothing. 'Open the suitcases,' ordered Hamish. Jessie slowly produced the keys. Hamish searched one of Jessie's pale-blue suitcases carefully after examining the passports. Their passports, which showed they were married, had been issued only a few weeks before.

Then he found the contract for the book and sheets of headed paper, 'Jessie Maclean, Literary Agent.' He silently took Jessie's handbag from her and tipped out the contents. In it was a banker's draft for the money.

Jessie glared up at him after stuffing everything back into her bag and clutching it tight. 'That money's mine,' she said. 'I earned it. I wrote the book.'

Hamish put both hands on the other side of the table and leaned forward.

'What were you doing on Eileencraig the day Heather Todd was murdered?'

'You're daft!' screamed Jessie. 'You all saw me arrive. You can't keep me. Let me out of here . . .'

Hamish smiled and slowly straightened up. He turned round and took the bag he had brought out of the hairdressers' from Harriet. He turned back and opened it and edged out of the bag a handful of red hair, a wig.

Harriet reflected dizzily that she had read of people turning green but had never seen it before that moment. Jessie's face was an awful colour under the harsh glare of the strip lighting overhead.

She rounded on her husband. 'You stupid bastard!' she screamed. 'You told me you'd burnt it.' She tried to rake his face with her nails and was dragged off, still screaming, by the detectives to a corner of the room, where she suddenly subsided into noisy sobs.

'Well, Willie Macdonald?' demanded Hamish. 'You'd better tell all or you'll find yourself on a murder charge as well.'

'Don't tell him,' gulped Jessie between sobs.

'It wisnae anything to do wi' me,' said Willie, looking down at the table. 'Jessie told me the auld bag had written a book but didnae want anyone to know about it in case it got rejected, so she asked Jessie tae type it oot and put her name down as literary agent. Jessie thought it was a right load o' rubbish. Then she got a phone call frae New York offering her a half a million on behalf of her client. She thought the whole thing up hersel'. Naethin' tae dae wi' me. She telt me she killed her. She hid ootside that health farm and watched fur the opportunity.'

His thin, weak face suddenly looked up at Hamish in puzzlement. 'But how did ye find the wig? I burnt it, like she said, in a bin in the garden at the back o' her flat.'

'And so you probably did,' said Hamish pleasantly. 'This is a wig I bought at a hairdressers' on the road here.'

'You bastard,' whispered Jessie suddenly. 'I could have got away with it.'

One of the detectives read the charges. 'We'll take them back to headquarters and get their statements. We'd better get your statement as well, Macbeth.' He held out his hand. 'Detective Sergeant Peter Sinclair, Macbeth. It's been a pleasure watching ye work. But man, man, ye took a chance buying that wig.'

Hamish shook hands with him, and then, putting an arm around Harriet's shoulders, he followed police and prisoners outside to the car.

When they finally emerged from police headquarters, all the city bells were ringing. A drunk reeled past, red-eyed under the street lights. 'Happy New Year,' he shouted.

'And so it is,' said Hamish. He put his arms around Harriet and held her close and bent his head to kiss her. He finally raised his head and looked down at her curiously. She was stiff in his arms and she had only endured that kiss.

'I think,' said Harriet breathlessly, 'that we should call on Diarmuid.'

'Why?' demanded Hamish, made cross by rejection. 'The police'll have phoned him.'

'Well, it's New Year's Eve and I have a feeling

170

he'll be all alone. Did you notice the times we were there that the phone did not ring once? No-one calling to offer their condolences?'

'Very well, then,' said Hamish sulkily. 'But I can tell you this, Harriet. I wish he *had* done it.'

They couldn't get a cab, so Hamish went back into the police station and begged a lift in a squad car.

As he rang Diarmuid's doorbell and waited, hoping that the man wouldn't answer, he wondered why Harriet had disliked that kiss. She was attracted to him, he was sure of that. He was just about to turn away, relieved, when the hall light went on and then Diarmuid answered the door. He was wearing pale-blue silk pyjamas and a white satin dressing-gown with his initials monogrammed in gold on one pocket.

'Hamish and Harriet,' he exclaimed. 'How good of you to come. This is a terrible business. A terrible business. The police told me about it.'

'Have you no-one with you?' asked Harriet as they followed him up the stairs and into the sitting-room. Diarmuid lit the gas fire. 'No,' he said. 'It's with it being New Year's Eve. I phoned a few people but they were all busy. Can you tell me about it, Hamish? All I got from the police was that Jessie had murdered my wife and that they would be calling on me in the morning to take a statement.'

Hamish sat down. He looked curiously at Harriet, a question in his eyes. She flushed slightly and looked away.

'It's like this,' said Hamish in a flat voice. 'Your wife wrote a steamy romance . . .'

'Heather? She never would!'

'I don't think she thought of it as popular writing,' said Harriet. 'She probably set out to write a literary novel and that's the way it came out. She must have read an awful lot of that kind of book, and with enjoyment, too. You can't really write what you don't like to read.'

Diarmuid put a finger to his brow and frowned. Does the man never stop acting? thought Hamish angrily.

'She did read a lot of them,' he volunteered, 'but it was because she said she was writing a speech to give to the Workers' Party on decadence and the decline of moral standards in popular fiction.'

What had Heather really been like under all that political pose? wondered Harriet. She must have needed a fantasy life to read and enjoy and absorb so many sexy romances.

'Anyway,' said Hamish, anxious to get this visit over with quickly, 'the police telephoned the owner of The Highland Comfort this evening. Jessie, padded out and wearing a red wig, just walked in about two weeks before the murder. She said she wanted a working holiday and he was glad to get her. No, he didn't ask for her employment card. He told the police that Jessie had told him her employment card was being sent on. He said Jane had spoiled things for him by paying high wages. He paid abysmal wages, as it turned out, so the island women who used to work for him preferred

172

to wait until the season started and work for Jane.'

'What name did Jessie use when she was working there?' asked Harriet.

'That's where I could kick myself,' said Hamish ruefully. 'She went under the name of Fiona Stuart, Heather's pseudonym.

'She said she didn't mean to murder Heather. She had some idea that if she told Heather, they could split the proceeds fifty-fifty, and she meant to suggest to her that they didn't let Diarmuid know. On her afternoon off, she hid behind that pillbox and saw us all coming out. Then she saw Heather and you, Diarmuid, having that row and Heather stalking off on her own. She followed her and when she considered they were both far enough away from the health farm, she caught up with her. Heather was amazed to see the efficient secretary, rising, it seemed, out of the moorland, wearing a red wig and with her cheeks and figure padded out.

'They walked together towards the west coast and that crag, and as they went, Jessie told Heather about her plan to split the proceeds. Heather was very excited, elated. She said her book was a literary work of art. She babbled on about possible lecture tours in the States. Jessie interrupted at last by asking her if they had a deal. Heather looked at her in surprise and said of course they hadn't a deal.

'Jessie then asked bitterly if she could at least depend on her agent's fee of fifteen per cent. Heather sneered that Jessie was nothing but a little secretary and was paid well for her duties and there was no need for her to get greedy. By this time she was standing on that crag. She looked out to sea and began to talk again about how famous she would be.

'Jessie said she suddenly thought of all the drudgery, all the work she had done for Heather, and she saw red. She saw a large, sharp rock lying on the ground at her feet. She picked it up and smashed it into the side of Heather's neck. Heather fell down on that little beach and lay still. Jessie threw the rock into the sea and ran all the way back to the hotel and waited until she heard the news next day that Heather's body had been found. She phoned you, Diarmuid, saying she was in Glasgow and you told her about Heather and she offered to come up. She was working in the bar that night and that was where you phoned to Angus Macleod to ask him to go and pick up Jessie. Jessie then approached Angus and said she was fed up with the hotel and wanted to leave, and as he was going to Oban anyway, he could take her.

'Once in Oban, she went to lodgings she had already hired and packed up the wig and the padding. Now the thing is, I do not think the murder was unpremeditated, because she had all the business papers and copies of Heather's will and insurance in a case already with her. All she had to do was travel back with Angus and then act the part of perfect secretary.'

'Did her husband put her up to it?' asked Harriet.

174

'Husband? What husband?' demanded Diarmuid.

'She had married a criminal, Willie Macdonald,' said Hamish. 'He had just got out of prison after serving a sentence for defrauding the company he had worked for as an accountant. He would know about cashing bank drafts and everything like that. But no, Jessie was the sole planner of the whole thing.'

'Goodness,' said Diarmuid weakly, 'and to think I have had a murderess working for me!'

Suddenly he leaned forward and said eagerly, 'Heather left me everything in her will. Of course, up till now "everything" was nothing but debts. Will I get the money for the book?'

Hamish looked at him with distaste. 'Oh, yes,' he said.

'And although all this publicity will be very painful,' put in Harriet, 'it should help sales immensely.'

Diarmuid rubbed his hands. 'Just wait till I tell my friends.'

'Yes, now you've money, you'll probably see them all again,' said Hamish cynically, but Diarmuid wasn't listening.

He crossed to the bar. 'Well,' he said cheerfully, 'this does call for a celebration.'

Hamish felt he had had enough. 'No, we must go. Coming, Harriet?'

Harriet stood up reluctantly. Hamish was going to ask her questions she didn't want to answer.

They walked silently together to their hotel. This time, Hamish followed Harriet into her room and looked down at her seriously. 'I am not in the way of making passes when I think they will not be welcome,' said Hamish. 'So what happened?'

'Sit down, Hamish,' said Harriet. Hamish sat on the edge of the bed and she sat beside him and took one of his hands in hers.

'I'm to blame.' Harriet looked up at him and there was the glitter of tears in her large grey eyes. 'I was . . . I am attracted to you. I should have let you know before, but it was all so exciting, the murder investigation, I mean.'

'Let me know what?'

'I am engaged to be married. My future husband, Neil, is an officer in the British Army. He's due back from Hong Kong.'

Hamish removed his hand. 'When?'

'In London, tomorrow. I'm travelling down on the morning plane.'

'You might have let me know,' said Hamish stiffly.

'Oh, Hamish . . .'

He rose. 'I, too, will leave in the morning,' he said without looking at her. 'Thank you for all your generosity and help.'

'Hamish . . .'

But he walked out and closed the door behind him.

He went to his room and set the alarm in case he slept in. He would catch the train to Edinburgh in the morning and from there take the train to

Inverness. He lay down on the bed, fully dressed, and tried not to feel like a fool.

And then the phone beside his ear rang sharp and insistent. He reached out and picked it up.

'Hamish!' came Priscilla Halburton-Smythe's voice.

'Priscilla.' He sat up.

'I've been phoning and phoning,' cried Priscilla. 'Where have you been?'

'Out. It's a long story. What's wrong?'

'I just wanted to wish you a Happy New Year.'

'Oh, aye, Happy New Year, Priscilla. Still with my folks?'

'No, back at the hotel. Towser's here. He's fine but missing you. I had the best Christmas ever. When do you get back?'

'I'm catching the Inverness train from Edinburgh tomorrow. I'll be in Inverness just after eight. I'll probably stay the night with my friends, Iain and Biddy, out at Torgormack, and then catch the sprinter in the morning.'

There was a silence and then Priscilla said, 'I'll come and fetch you if you like. Tomorrow. At Inverness station.'

'That would be grand, Priscilla.'

There was another silence.

Then Priscilla's voice, sharp and anxious. 'What's up, Hamish?'

'It wass the end of a murder inquiry,' said Hamish. 'I feel flat. I'll tell you all about it when I see you.'

'How come you are staying at such an expensive hotel? Glasgow police being generous?'

'No, I'll tell you about that as well. I'd better get some sleep.'

'All right, Hamish. Goodbye.'

Priscilla slowly replaced the receiver. Something had happened to Hamish Macbeth and she was sure it was nothing to do with the murder case he had been on.

CHAPTER EIGHT

Good breeding consists in concealing
how much we think of ourselves and how
little we think of the other person.
—MARK TWAIN

The tinny alarm bell shrilled in Hamish's ear and he started up. He had fallen asleep still dressed, and he felt hot and dirty. He had a shower and changed and then went along to Harriet's room and tapped on the door.

He felt he had behaved very badly. She had not thrown herself at him. He had read too much into simple friendliness and he had no right to be angry with her.

There was no reply to his knock and all at once he knew she had left. He looked at his watch. Seven in the morning.

He went down to the reception desk. The night porter, still on duty, answered his query by saying that, yes, she had left. There was a letter for him. Hamish glanced at it. He could not bear to read it and shoved it into his pocket.

He had breakfast and then packed and made his way to the station to catch the Edinburgh train, stopping off on the way to buy a bottle of perfume for Priscilla. He felt he should have gone to visit his relatives and stayed with them in Glasgow for another night, but could not bring himself to do so. Before boarding the train, he bought the morning papers. The news of the arrest of Jessie and her husband had occurred too late for the first editions. He wondered if he would be mentioned in the later editions and then decided, probably not. Glasgow police would take the credit, not out of vanity, but simply to avoid long-winded explanations to the press about how some holidaying Highland copper came to solve the mystery.

He had had very little sleep and nodded off, only waking when a shout of 'Waverley, next stop!' heralded his arrival in Edinburgh.

A group raising money for famine relief were singing Christmas carols in a corner of the station. It seemed almost indecent to hear Christmas carols in the new year.

Hamish lugged his travelling-bag to the Inverness train. Every seat was taken and he had to stand as far as Stirling. When he was finally seated, he remembered Harriet's letter and reluctantly pulled it out. 'Dear Hamish,' he read. 'Do not think too badly of me. I should have told you at the beginning that I was engaged. It was all my fault. I am sorry our great adventure had to end this way and please don't feel too badly rejected. Think of me sometimes. I shall certainly never forget you. Love, Harriet.'

He shrugged and put the letter back in his pocket. As the towns slid past on the road to the north, Perth, Blair Atholl, Dalwhinnie, Kingussie, Aviemore, he felt the whole business receding. Eileencraig with Jane and her health farm, Geordie and his truck seemed a million miles away. He wondered briefly if Jane and John Wetherby would remarry.

And then he arrived in Inverness. Snow was falling as he walked along the platform, the sea-gulls of Inverness were screaming overhead, and there was Priscilla, standing at the end of the platform with Towser on a leash.

She dropped the leash and Towser came bounding up to meet him, ridiculous tail wagging energetically, scrabbling at Hamish in delight with large muddy paws.

'He looks well,' said Hamish, dropping a kiss on Priscilla's cold cheek, 'and so do you.' She was almost restored to her former beauty. Her golden hair had a healthy shine and the hollows had left her cheeks.

'Your mother's cooking,' said Priscilla. 'I was going to take you out to dinner in Inverness, and then I thought you would probably like to go straight home.'

'Aye, that would be grand,' said Hamish, his face lighting up in a smile.

'So,' said Priscilla as she drove the hotel Range Rover out over the bridge and took the road to the north, 'tell me about the case.'

Hamish began, reluctantly at first, and then all at once he was back on Eileencraig. He described all the guests vividly, with the exception of Harriet Shaw.

'And so you went to Glasgow,' said Priscilla, 'and stayed at that expensive little hotel. Unlike you, Hamish. Hamish?'

'I wasnae paying,' mumbled Hamish.

'And who was?'

'Harriet Shaw.'

'So you were a kept man,' commented Priscilla coolly. 'What was she like?'

'Who?'

'*Hamish!*'

'Well, nice, ordinary, straightforward. Writes cookery books.'

'I know, I have several of her books. She's very good. What prompted the generous offer, or should I ask?'

'She wass helping me wi' my inquiries,' said Hamish stiffly. 'If she hadn't volunteered to pay, I couldn't even have afforded a more modest hotel.'

'You could have stayed with Jean,' pointed out Priscilla, an edge to her voice.

Hamish cursed under his breath. Of course, after a stay with his family, Priscilla would know the names of all his relatives.

'Look,' he said, 'it chust happened. She was helping me wi' my inquiries.'

'Oh, yes,' said Priscilla flatly. 'How old is she?'

'About forty-five.'

'As old as that? And where is she now?'

'Gone to meet her fiancé in London.'

'Oh.' There was a long pause. Then Priscilla said cheerfully, 'I remember seeing her on television. Pleasant-looking woman. Certainly looks a lot younger than forty-five.'

'Not when you meet her,' said Hamish, thrusting a knife into his memory of Harriet in order to keep the atmosphere between himself and Priscilla light.

'Well, it's all very odd,' remarked Priscilla.

'What is?' demanded Hamish, hoping she would not pursue his relationship with Harriet Shaw any further.

'This Heather Todd, the one who was killed. Imagine writing a whole novel and your husband not even knowing about it.'

'He said she was always scribbling at something and he thought she was preparing a speech for the Workers' Party.'

'Still, to keep up that Communist front and yet relish reading romances. A sort of double life. Perhaps she is to be pitied.'

'You didn't meet her,' said Hamish. 'She was a nasty, irritating woman. When I told her I was in forestry because I didn't want her to know I was a policeman, she hectored me about the destruction of the environment until I began to want to see the whole world covered in concrete. She had that sort of effect. She was a woman begging to be murdered.'

'That's what I meant,' said Priscilla. 'Surely to

be pitied. And Jane? Are all her friends like me, mere acquaintances?'

'So it seems.'

'And have you thought about that rock that Jane said nearly killed her?'

'No, why?' Hamish sounded puzzled. 'I took a good look at the bathroom heater and decided the builder had been right. It was an accident, so I never got around to asking her closely about the rock or bothering to see where it had happened.'

'Think of it this way,' said Priscilla as they drove over the Dornoch Firth bridge, 'Heather liked to dress like Jane. Jessie was no doubt prowling the island on her time off long before the day of the murder, waiting for an opportunity to get rid of Heather. There's little daylight this time of year. She could have seen Jane in the darkness, mistaken her for Heather, and shied a rock at her. Now if that had happened, and she had succeeded in killing Jane, it would really have complicated things.'

'I should have questioned that further,' said Hamish ruefully. 'In fact, I've been verra lucky all round. If Harriet Shaw hadn't been there, and herself an author to let me know all about the selling of books, and if Jessie hadn't cracked at the sight of that red wig, it would have been difficult to prove. But the biggest mistake of all was not asking at the hotel what name the maid had used. Can you imagine? Jessie used the name Fiona Stuart, Heather's pseudonym.'

'But even if you had found out earlier, it

wouldn't have meant a thing,' pointed out Priscilla. 'It wouldn't have meant anything unless you had got the idea about the book.'

'That's true,' agreed Hamish. 'But what about you, Priscilla? I'm surprised you stayed with my family for so long.'

'I had the best Christmas I've ever had, Hamish.' Priscilla left the main road and drove the car expertly towards the Struie Pass. 'So easygoing. Such fun. And your mother is a darling.'

'What about Aunt Hannah?'

'Well, that's the odd thing. She was quite miffed that you weren't there and felt you had deliberately snubbed her.'

'That's her way,' said Hamish. 'She always did like making people feel guilty.'

'But she didn't manage to spoil the fun. I slept for hours and hours and ate huge meals, played Scrabble and Monopoly, went for walks with your brothers and sisters, and went to the pub with your father. You are lucky, Hamish. I often wish I had brothers and sisters.'

'You'll have children of your own one day,' said Hamish. There was a sudden constraint between them and they drove most of the rest of the way back to Lochdubh in silence.

When they were driving along the waterfront at Lochdubh, Priscilla said awkwardly, 'You left me the keys, so I took the liberty of preparing a meal for us.'

'That was kind of you. Thank you.'

Towser frolicked before them into the kitchen

and stood wagging his tail next to the cooker and looking up at them hopefully. 'I'd better feed the dog first,' said Priscilla. 'You go through the living-room, Hamish, and put your feet up. The fire's made up. All you have to do is put a match to it.'

Hamish took off his coat and hung it up. He went into the living-room and lit the fire. Then he remembered he had bought Priscilla a bottle of perfume before boarding the train in Glasgow and was glad he had done so because there was a pile of Christmas presents from his family lying on the table and also one with a card that he recognized from the handwriting as being from Priscilla.

'I've got you a present,' he shouted. 'It's in my coat pocket.'

'Thank you, Hamish.' Priscilla went to his coat, which was hanging behind the back door, and felt in the pockets and then pulled out a small square box. As she did so, a crumpled piece of paper fell out and dropped to the floor. She picked it up and automatically smoothed it out. It was Harriet's letter to Hamish. She shouldn't have read it, but she did.

So, thought Priscilla, reading between the lines, Hamish made a pass, and a heavy one, too.

'Like it?' called Hamish.

'What?' Priscilla feverishly tore off the wrapping paper from the present. 'Yes. Lovely. My favourite French perfume.' She carefully put the crumpled letter back in his pocket. Towser was eating with relish, his tail still wagging, delighted to be home.

With nervous efficient movements, Priscilla

grilled a steak, fried potatoes, mushrooms, and tomatoes, put the lot on a tray and carried it through.

'I'm being fair spoiled,' said Hamish with a grin. Then he said, 'Where's yours?'

'I'm not really hungry,' said Priscilla, 'and I've just remembered I have a lot to do. I'd better go.'

'Oh, can't you stay for a bit? I thought Johnson was handling everything.'

'No, no. Must run. 'Bye, Hamish.' And she fairly ran from the room and the next minute he heard the kitchen door slam.

He felt very flat. He had not even opened his presents.

Women!

THE END

M. C. Beaton started her career in Glasgow as a fiction buyer for John Smith bookshop. She has worked for a number of leading newspapers and magazines, including the *Scottish Daily Express*, and the *Daily Express* in Fleet Street, where she was Chief Woman Reporter. She also worked for Rupert Murdoch's *Star* newspaper in America and was a freelance writer for the *New York Daily News*.

She began writing historical novels in 1978 and launched her highly successful Hamish Macbeth series in 1985, after which she rapidly became a cult figure in America. When she returned to Britain, she lived on a croft in Sutherland and then moved south to the Cotswolds, where she now lives in a Georgian cottage with her husband Harry and son Charles.

DEATH OF A HUSSY
by M. C. Beaton

A HAMISH MACBETH MYSTERY

The scenic Highland town of Lochdubh has been shaken up by the arrival of Maggie Baird, a hefty and tweed-loving Englishwoman who is determined to become the town's leading lady. But Police Constable Hamish Macbeth – renowned for his sleepy style of policing – is not fooled by her matronly façade, and his intuition proves correct when she mysteriously disappears, and then returns a few months later newly svelte, sleek, and ready to start entertaining a stream of seedy suitors. But before her transformation pays off with a marriage proposal, Maggie is murdered and crime has indeed hit Lochdubh, leading Hamish on a trail marked with passion and greed as he works to discover the truth behind the death of a hussy.

A Bantam Paperback

0 553 40967 0

DEATH OF A GLUTTON
by M. C. Beaton

A HAMISH MACBETH MYSTERY

Peta Gore is the bane of her partner's otherwise successful life. Trying to work with Peta on a matchmaking business that Peta uses mostly for her own purposes, Maria Worth has come to hate her old friend, a noisy, vulgar glutton. But this time Maria is determined to keep her latest singles' event a secret from Peta. The gathering is to be at Tommel Castle Hotel in the remote Scottish village of Lochdubh, the perfect setting for a particularly difficult group. Nothing can go wrong. Except that somehow Peta finds out about the gathering and shows up, thoroughly disgusting everyone. Guests and staff band together in mutual loathing. But does someone hate her enough to kill her?

A Bantam Paperback

0 553 40972 7

DEATH OF A PRANKSTER
by M. C. Beaton

A HAMISH MACBETH MYSTERY

When Police Constable Hamish Macbeth receives the news that there has been a murder at Arrat House, home of the relentless practical joker Arthur Trent, previous experience leads him to suspect that this is no more than another prank. But when he arrives, he finds that Trent is most decidedly dead, having been stabbed and stuffed in a closet. For suspects, there is a houseful of greedy relations, all of whom are more interested in the contents of the will than in the crime at hand. To complicate matters further, Chief Inspector Blair, Hamish's old nemesis, arrives on the scene as determined as ever to stand in the way of Macbeth's investigation. When his former flame, Priscilla Halburton-Smythe, gets involved as well, Hamish quite nearly has his hands full. Accordingly, the charming constable must enliven his sleepy style of detecting – and M. C. Beaton once again offers up a witty and well-crafted mystery peopled with quirky characters and a most endearing sleuth.

A Bantam Paperback

0 553 40967 9

A SELECTION OF CRIME AND MYSTERY NOVELS AVAILABLE FROM BANTAM BOOKS

40791	0	**DEATH OF A GOSSIP**	*M. C. Beaton* £3.99
40792	9	**DEATH OF A CAD**	*M. C. Beaton* £3.99
40793	7	**DEATH OF AN OUTSIDER**	*M. C. Beaton* £3.99
40794	5	**DEATH OF A PERFECT WIFE**	*M. C. Beaton* £3.99
40967	0	**DEATH OF A HUSSY**	*M. C. Beaton* £3.99
40968	9	**DEATH OF A SNOB**	*M. C. Beaton* £3.99
40967	9	**DEATH OF A PRANKSTER**	*M. C. Beaton* £3.99
40972	7	**DEATH OF A GLUTTON**	*M. C. Beaton* £3.99
40795	3	**PERFECT COVER**	
		Linda Chase & Joyce St George £4.99	
40922	0	**THE JUROR**	*George Dawes Green* £5.99
17676	5	**PEOPLE LIKE US**	*Dominick Dunne* £4.99
17189	5	**THE TWO MRS GRENVILLES**	*Dominick Dunne* £3.50
40321	4	**AN INCONVENIENT WOMAN**	*Dominick Dunne* £4.99
40400	8	**A SEASON IN PURGATORY**	*Dominick Dunne* £4.99
40937	9	**YESTERDAY'S PAPERS**	*Martin Edwards* £3.99
40237	4	**FOR THE SAKE OF ELENA**	*Elizabeth George* £4.99
40167	X	**WELL-SCHOOLED IN MURDER**	
		Elizabeth George £4.99	
17510	6	**A GREAT DELIVERANCE**	*Elizabeth George* £4.99
17511	4	**PAYMENT IN BLOOD**	*Elizabeth George* £4.99
40845	3	**PLAYING FOR THE ASHES**	*Elizabeth George* £4.99
40168	8	**A SUITABLE VENGEANCE**	*Elizabeth George* £4.99
40238	2	**MISSING JOSEPH**	*Elizabeth George* £4.99
40259	5	**LAST RIGHTS**	*Tim Sebastian* £4.99
40796	1	**FINNEGAN'S WEEK**	*Joseph Wambaugh* £4.99